LOVING HIM AIN'T WORTH A DAMN

PART TWO

BY

RACQUEL WILLIAMS

Copyright

Publisher's Note: This is a work of fiction. Any resemblance to actual persons (living or dead), or references to real people, events, songs, business establishments or locales is purely coincidental. All characters are fictional, and all events are imaginative. LOVING HIM AIN'T WORTH A DAMN PART 2

Copyright © 2017 Author: **Racquel Williams**

Publisher: **RACQUEL WILLIAMS PRESENTS**

Acknowledgements

I want to give all praises to Allah. Without him I wouldn't be able to do the things that I love to do, writing included.

Shout out to everyone that has been rocking with me from day and still rocking with me. I appreaciate y'all.

Shout out to my support system. There are days when I want to give up, but y'all push me and encourage me to keep on grinding. I love y'all.

PROLOGUE

Amoy

I felt a lump in my throat as I tried to find the words to say to my little sister. The one that I took care of my entire life... How could she do this to me? Me, her big sister and protector... I sold my pussy when I was younger to help buy food for her ass when she was hungry. I bought soap, so she was able to wash her dirty ass, and this was how she repaid me?

"Sis, this is not what it seems," this snake ass bitch had the nerve to say to me.

"Yo, what the fuck you mean, bitch? I just heard my nigga... fuck that, the father of your nephew, call you 'babe', and you're telling me, this is not what it seems? My dear loving sister, please explain this shit to me." I rested my baby's car seat on the ground because I was ready to rip this little bitch's head off.

"Man, come on, B. You've got my seed and shit right here. Just go ahead on home. Your sister told you it's not what you think, but yet, you're up in here, trying to start some fucking drama."

I turned my head to face this fuck nigga. I took a few steps toward him. "Really, Devon, you're defending this little bitch? Okay, since you're speaking up and shit, tell me how long you've been fucking with this bitch?"

"Man, go ahead with all that. I'll be over there later on."

"You're a bitch, just like this hoe. You're not even man enough to claim this hoe in front of me."

I then turned to this bitch and looked at her with disgust written all on my face.

"This is what you wanted? My leftovers, a no good ass nigga with a fucking wife? You're not even the second bitch but the third bitch. I swear, I should beat your motherfucking ass for even trying me." I lunged towards this bitch.

"I just told your motherfucking ass that you need to take my son and go the fuck home. I mean, what kind of example are you setting for him?"

"Nigga, quit claiming that little bastard. I told your ass you need a DNA test 'cause my lovely sister here doesn't know who the fuck her baby daddy is."

"Is this true, Amoy? Is he some other nigga's seed?" Devon turned around to face me.

I couldn't believe what this bitch just opened her mouth to say. I was really stuck and lost for words. I was angry, but I was more hurt; it was like broken glass was digging into an open wound. As much as I wanted to pretend that this was a stranger, it wasn't. This was my blood, my little sister that was doing this to me.

"You know what? Fuck you and this bitch. I swear my motherfucking son don't need you any motherfucking way."

Loving Him Ain't Worth A Damn Part 2

"Nah, fuck that. Is this my son or not? What the fuck is your sister talking about?" He grabbed my arm tightly.

"Let go of my fucking arm unless you're trying to get a new fucking charge," I snapped at him and snatched my arm away.

I turned around, grabbed my baby's seat, opened the door, and stormed out of there as fast as my legs would carry me.

I strapped my son into his car seat while I tried my hardest to control my emotions. I got into my seat and put my seatbelt on. My hands trembled as I put them on the steering wheel. I wasted no time getting out of there. As soon as I pulled off, the tears rushed out of my eyes, like a dam that was broken. I was shocked and hurt... not so much behind that nigga but behind that little bitch back there that called herself my sister.

Who the fuck raised this bitch? I thought. Then reality hit me; our mama was trifling as fuck, and she was the one responsible for raising this little bitch. How could I expect any different? The shit caught me off guard though. How could I be so blind and miss the signs, or did I see them but was too blind to believe them? My mind was clouded, and my emotions were running wild. I tried to stop the tears, but they wouldn't stop. The more that I thought about what had just popped off, the angrier I got.

Fuck that nigga, but my little sister... How could she let dick come between us? Not just any dick but a nigga that was married? A nigga that could possibly be the father to her blood?

3

Racquel Williams

I busted a U-turn in the middle of the street. I was furious, and I needed some fucking answers. I had a strong feeling that this crack head bitch knew about this all along, and there was only one way to find out. Tears continued pouring down my face as my heart continued to break.

I got out of my car and got my baby out of his seat. That damn car seat was too heavy to carry up the stairs. I sped up the stairs while holding my baby close to me. My adrenaline was rushing, which gave me a new wave of energy.

I banged loudly on her door while I waited impatiently.

"Who the fuck is banging on my door like that?" she yelled out loud.

"Mama, it's me. Amoy. Open the door."

"What the fuck you want? Last time I was all kinds of hoes and shit."

I saw I was going to get nowhere with this bitch if I went at her aggressively.

"I brought your grandson to see you. You know you ain't seen him."

I waited for a response. Seconds later, I heard the bolts of the door moving. She opened the door.

I pushed past her and entered her apartment. "So, did you know Shari was fucking my baby daddy?"

Loving Him Ain't Worth A Damn Part 2

"Say what? Is this what you came over here for?" She looked at me.

"Answer me, bitch. Did you know your whorish daughter was fucking my son's father? Did you put her up to it?"

"Listen to me, you little bitch. I don't give a fuck if you're holding my grandbaby or not; I will tear that ass up. Don't come up in my shit, accusing me of anything. You know yo ass been jealous of Shari ever since I brought her home from the hospital. I never understood why until now."

"Jealous of her? Bitch, I took care of her ass because your crackhead ass was out fucking and sucking on any nigga that could support your crack and dope habit. But you don't remember that shit. Bitch, you know I'm tired of sparing your fucking feelings. I should've known you weren't shit when you stayed wit' the nigga that fucked yo daughters. What kind of fucking mother are you? Wait, I know. You're a sorry piece of shit. I promise I wish you were dead, bitch. Matter-of-fact, I can't wait for your ass to be dead, so I can spit on your fucking grave."

"Ha ha, you've been dead to me. I should've aborted yo ass when that sperm donor begged me to. And just for the record, Richard didn't rape you like you claimed. Yo little fast ass wanted that dick. Matter-of-fact, you were jealous of me getting that good dick every night. So, you threw yo little dumb ass all over him. You're just mad 'cause he fucked you and didn't want anything else to do with your dirty ass."

"Fuck you," I said in a cold tone.

I looked that bitch up and down. It was a waste of my time to even be here around her. I shook my head and then turned around and walked out. She was so strung out and looked pitiful. The door slammed behind me. I could still hear that bitch yelling and screaming. I didn't look back. I exited the building and walked to my car. I strapped my baby back into his seat. The good thing was that he managed to stay asleep through all the drama.

With fucking family like this, who the fuck needs enemies? This bitch should have never had kids, much less called herself a mother. I'm done with both them bitches; I swear on my seed, I thought as I pulled off.

Loving Him Ain't Worth A Damn Part 2

CHAPTER ONE

Shari

Lord knows I was not ready for this drama that unfolded in my apartment earlier. When I opened that door, I wasn't ready to see my sister's face. I tried to get her to leave, but this bitch busted her ass up in my shit, and there it was. Her baby daddy was there, in the middle of my apartment, with only his boxers on.

Shit, I wasn't going to lie; after the shock disappeared, I was happy on the inside when I saw how angry that bitch was. Yes, this bitch acted like her shit didn't stink, but her nigga was caught in another woman's apartment. I would do anything to find out what was going through her mind.

This bitch should've just grabbed her little bastard and left. Instead, her dumb ass stuck around, trying to come at me. So, being the proud bitch that I was, I gave it to her ass. Her eyes popped out when I told the nigga that wasn't his seed. What the fuck did she expect? I was going to let my nigga take care of a baby that possibly wasn't his?

After she left out, I walked over and locked my door. All that fucking drama was not necessary. She acted like this was the first time a nigga done cheated on her ass. That was what her dumb ass got for believing in these niggas.

"So you're married? This old, stupid bitch has no idea that I know this already." I burst out laughing.

"She thought she was telling you some shit you didn't already know. Maybe trying to get you to leave me alone."

For some strange reason, I was kind of heated that he was still married to that bitch, and he had a smirk on his face. I stared at him and was kind of irritated. I was going to trip out on that nigga, show him how much of a savage I really was. I quickly caught myself. I wasn't into the drama. I was the chick that provided him with the calm in this crazy world. Truth was, I didn't give a fuck that he was fucking my sister, so why the fuck would I care that he was married to a bitch only on paper? Bitches really didn't know me, but they would soon.

"Aiight, babe. I'm so sorry this bitch popped up like that."

"Nah, bae, you're good. I'm the one that's sorry. I didn't mean to bring no drama to your house. I know she's your sister and all, and I would never want to come between y'all relationship. I understand if you 'ont want to fuck wit' a nigga anymore."

"Say what? Yo, fuck that bitch. Blood don't make us family. You're my fucking family. I regret that you didn't move out the way, so I could show that bitch these hands. She will soon realize that I'm no longer a little ass girl but a grown ass woman that's fucking her nigga," I said in a cold tone.

"Well, fuck her for real. Come on; let Daddy show you how much he appreciates you." He grabbed my hand and pulled me towards the bedroom.

Loving Him Ain't Worth A Damn Part 2

Devon and I fucked for about an hour. That nigga ate my pussy and my asshole like he was famished. I thought I was freaky; shit, this nigga beat me at being a freak. I wasn't complaining though. I loved it.

After we finished fucking, we took a shower, and I cooked us some French fries and chicken nuggets. See, I wasn't going to front like I was a big time cook. Shit, who the fuck was there to teach me to cook? Both of them bitches were too busy being whores, but shit, he wasn't complaining. Matter-of-fact, he ate that shit like it was the best meal he'd ever had.

"Aye, bae, I'm about to make a few runs."

I whipped my head around so damn fast. "Where you going?"

"About to handle some business. You know money goin' get low, so I need to get back in these streets."

My face lit up when he said that. I was happy that baby boy knew that pussy wasn't free, and if he wanted to fuck with me, he needed to have some fucking money. Shit, like Kanye West said, "I ain't saying I'm a gold digger, but I ain't messin' wit' no broke nigga."

"Okay, bae. Just be careful out there. You know you're out on bond."

"I know, yo. I'm good though."

After he got dressed, he kissed me on the cheek and left out. I locked the door behind him. I decided to do the dishes, so I could be free the rest of the evening. As I washed the dishes, my mind ran back on the situation that popped off earlier. I was confused why my sister

9

popped up over here out of the blue. How did she suspect that I was fucking with her baby daddy?

I rocked my brain, trying to come up with these answers. Only three people knew about our relationship. That was me, Devon, and that bitch, Kaysia. That was when it hit me. That bitch and I got into it a few days ago because she was jealous of me and Devon's relationship.

"You dirty bitch," I said out loud.

I cut off the water and dried my hands. I walked off into my room to retrieve my cellphone. My hands trembled as I pulled that bitch's number up and hit call.

"Hello."

"Bitch, who the fuck did you tell I was fucking with Devon?"

"First off, bitch, don't call my phone with no damn drama."

"Answer my fucking question, Kaysia. Did you tell my stupid ass sister that I was fucking her baby daddy?"

"You know what, Shari? Matter-of-fact, I sure did. I mean, if you're woman enough to fuck her man, you should be able to take that ass whopping like a grown bitch."

"Both of you bitches are silly! I ain't met the bitch yet that can whup my ass, but you already know that. Shit, all you did was hurt that bitch's feelings, not mine."

"You're a cold-hearted ass bitch. I can't believe I ever fucked with you, but you know karma is right around the corner, bitch."

Loving Him Ain't Worth A Damn Part 2

Before I could respond, that bitch hung up in my face. I immediately tried to call back because I wasn't done addressing this dike ass bitch. Her phone kept going to voicemail. Old scary ass bitch, her and my sister would do good as friends. Both of them bitches were scary as fuck.

That bitch blew my motherfucking nerves. I couldn't believe that bitch would do me like that. She was my nigga, my road dawg. Damn, this bitch let jealousy come between our friendship. Oh well, fuck that hoe now.

I grabbed a bag of weed that I had in my purse. I quickly rolled it up and took a few drags. I needed to calm myself down. These bitches had no idea that I wasn't your average bitch, and I would snap on their asses.

Racquel Williams

KENNEDY

I woke up bright and early. I had an appointment to see a divorce lawyer. Yes, you heard me right, a fucking divorce lawyer. At first, I thought about working it out with my two-timing husband, but the more I thought about his behavior, the more I realized that I couldn't control this nigga and his cheating ways. Not only was he cheating, but he had the audacity to bring a little bastard into this world. Yeah, the nigga denied it, but I didn't believe a word that came out of his flipping mouth. I was even more upset that he brought that bitch into my house. That nigga had no respect at all for me, and it was showing in his actions.

I parked my car and got out. My heart was heavy, no sense for me to pretend that I was happy about doing this. I'd already lost one husband, and now I was about to walk away from another. *My luck with men*, I thought.

I breathed a long sigh of relief and walked into the building.

"Good morning. I'm here to see Attorney Bajan."

"Good morning, and your name please?"

"Kennedy Guthrie."

"Have a seat please, and I'll let him know you're here."

I took a seat in the corner. I was trying my best not to think about Devon and his bad behavior.

"Mrs. Guthrie, he's ready to see you now. The first door on the right." She pointed in that direction.

12

Loving Him Ain't Worth A Damn Part 2

I knocked on the door before I entered. "Mrs. Guthrie, nice to meet you. Sit down."

"Nice meeting you also."

"Alrighty, let's get down to business. I know we spoke briefly over the phone, but can you tell me a little more about your husband and what brings you to this point?"

I started airing out mine and Devon's dirty laundry to this stranger. At times, I paused as I thought about the roller coaster ride that this nigga had taken me on lately.

"Wow! It seems like you've been through hell with him. Okay, do you have any emails, text messages, pictures, receipts? Anything that can help your case against him. We can file the divorce based on adultery. Do you all have any children?"

"No, we didn't."

"Good, does your husband have any off-shore accounts, real estate, or businesses that you know about?"

"That bastard has nothing. He came in this relationship with nothing but the drawers on his ass. Please excuse my language."

"No, you're fine. I am concerned that the court will grant him half of your estate."

"Say what? I'm not giving his ass shit. I done took care of this bastard, and now you're telling me I might have to give up my shit that my late husband left me?"

Racquel Williams

"No, not the things you had before the marriage but everything that was acquired during the marriage. I'm pretty sure he'll be getting a lawyer also that will be asking for spousal support since you're the one that supported him."

"Bullshit! I'll be damned if I'm going to keep taking care of a grown ass man that is slinging dick all over town. Excuse my French." I stood up.

My blood was boiling as I digested what this man was saying to me.

"I'm only letting you know what to expect under New York's law."

"So, you mean to tell me that this nigga can run around town, slinging dick from bitch to bitch, and I need to pay him? Over my dead body," I said before I took a seat.

"I'm your attorney, and I'm here to fight for you. I'm only telling you these things so you can know what to expect. Divorce proceedings can get downright messy sometimes. I just want you to be prepared."

I sat there, thinking. I wondered if there was a way I could get away with murder. I mean, this wasn't the first time that I'd killed a no good ass nigga, but the question was could I pull it off again?

"Mrs. Guthrie." His voice startled me, bringing me back to reality.

"Yes, I'm sorry."

"I was asking if you want me to go ahead and start the divorce proceedings?"

Loving Him Ain't Worth A Damn Part 2

"Uh, umm. You know what? Give me a few days; let me reconsider this. It might be cheaper to stay married."

"Sure, take all the time you need. I'm going to keep your file, so when you're ready, we can jump right on it."

"Thank you so much. I'll be in touch soon."

"Great. Have a good day."

I didn't know what my crazy ass was thinking, but I hauled ass out of there. I got in my car and sat down for a few minutes before pulling off. See, it wasn't that I didn't want to divorce him; I just wanted to weigh my options first. There was no way that I was giving his two-timing ass a dime of my got damn money.

***

I decided to invite Christopher over for dinner. He had been so good to me lately, and whenever I called, he was always there. I knew he was in love with me; he just wasn't my type. I guess you could say that he was a little more on the conservative side. That didn't stop me from using him to do whatever it was that I wanted.

I decided to throw a roast in the oven. I also cooked rice with broccoli, and I baked a chocolate cake. I sure missed throwing down in the kitchen, but since I was home by myself, there was no reason for me to cook every day.

Tonight was different though. I planned on enjoying the evening with Christopher in every way possible. After the dinner was cooked, I checked the time; it was a quarter past seven. Dinner was at 8 P.M., so

Racquel Williams

I had time to jump in the shower and get myself together before he got here.

The entire time that I was bathing, I tried my hardest not to think about Devon. Just thinking about him and how he disrespected me only made me hate him. All kinds of wicked thoughts were running through my head. I shook the thoughts away and washed off with cold water. Yes, you heard me right. I learned a long time ago that hot water wrinkled the skin, and there was no way I wanted to walk around with saggy looking skin; I didn't give a damn how old I was.

I got out of the shower, dried off, and lotioned my body down with the new Oil of Olay lotion. I glanced in the mirror. I looked damn good for my age. I ran my hands across my breasts that were sitting up pretty. I damn sure could give these young bitches a run for their money. Not only that, I knew my pussy was still tight and could grip a dick tight. That husband of mine was a damn fool because how could he walk away from all of this? I took one last glance and then slipped on my silk evening dress that I picked out just for this night. I then sprayed a little perfume around my ears. Now, I was ready to entertain this man.

I dished the food out and waited for him. Before I could sit down, I heard the doorbell ringing. *This man is always on time,* I thought before I got up to go answer the door.

I opened the door, and his fine ass was standing there with a red rose in his hand.

Loving Him Ain't Worth A Damn Part 2

"Hey there, beautiful. This is for you." He handed me the rose.

"Well, thank you, sir." I took it.

He stepped inside, and I locked the door behind us. "Damn, it smells good up in here. What the hell you got going on up in here?" he asked and walked towards the dining room.

"I hope you're hungry, love."

He sat down at the table, and I put a bottle of red wine and a bowl of ice in front of him.

"I know you're tired of me saying this, but woman, you can cook your ass off. Man, I wish I had a woman to cook these kinds of meals for me every night. Shit, I would never eat out."

"Well, you never know... If you play your cards right, you might just have these meals every night," I hinted.

"Talk to me, lady. What you saying?" He placed the fork down on the plate.

"Christopher, stop the nonsense. Eat up your food. We have plenty of time to talk about that."

"So, how did it go with the lawyer? Did you show him all the pics that I gave to you?"

He caught me off guard with that question.

"Yes, I went to see the lawyer, but I didn't retain him as of yet."

"I thought you were ready to get the ball rolling on the divorce."

"I am, but after he mentioned that the bastard might get half of my money, I had a change of heart."

"Change of heart?" He cut me off.

"Relax, Christopher. I just had a change of heart, just for now."

"Oh, okay."

I could tell he was a little bothered by what I said because his demeanor changed.

"I didn't invite you over to talk about that dog. Tonight is purely about us."

I got up from my side and walked over to him. I started massaging his shoulders. I then started kissing his neck.

"Woman, don't you start something you can't finish," he said and took a sip of his wine.

"I'm a grown ass woman, and if I see something that I want, then I'm definitely going to go after it." I continued kissing his neck while I started unbuttoning his collared shirt.

He put the glass down and got up from the chair. He stood up, grabbed my hands, and pulled me towards him. He locked his lips onto mine and started kissing me. He wasted no time in picking me up and carrying me to the couch. He was a bit aggressive, but who was I to complain? He put me down and took my silk dress off, leaving my breasts out in the open. He laid me on my back on the couch as he knelt down beside me, taking his hands and massaging my breasts. He then took one and placed it in his mouth. My body started to react to this man in a different way. He took his time, using his tongue to twirl around my nipple. He then reached down, with his other hand, and slid his two middle fingers into my pussy, which was soaking wet. I twitched as he worked my middle with his fingers. This man was working magic with my body without actually sexing me.

"Oweiii," I moaned out as I grinded on his fingers.

"Damn, baby. I want you," he whispered in my ear.

"So what you waiting on?"

I guess that was all he needed to hear because he started kissing my stomach and licking my navel. He then inhaled my pussy before he used his tongue to lick my clit. He then started kissing my pussy passionately. My body started shivering as I tried to control my emotions.

"Please, babes, fuck me," I screamed out to him.

He didn't pay me any mind. Instead, he sucked my clit like he was a pro on eating pussy. My legs started shivering as juice flooded out of my body and onto his face. He didn't move a muscle; instead, he used his tongue and licked all of my juices up. He then got up and took his pants off, revealing his hard dick. For a man of his build, I was looking for a halfway decent dick. Wrong. It was a little on the small side, even though it was hard. I quickly took my eyes off of it and turned my focus on him. He eased inside of me.

"Aweeee," I moaned out to give him a boost.

"Damn, baby, this pussy is good," he said as he dug deeper inside of me. He took my right leg and lifted it in the air. He then thrusted in and out of my slippery pussy. The dick might not be that big, but

Christopher knew how to work the pussy. He was no Devon in the bed, but he could definitely satisfy me for now, and I'd have him exactly where I wanted him.

"Damn, baby, I love you," he blurted out, shocking the hell out of me.

I didn't respond. Shit, I didn't know what the hell to say. I liked him, but as far as love, I couldn't say it back. He gripped me tighter as his veins got larger, and he started thrusting harder. I knew then that he was about to bust. His cum shot up in my pussy like a straight shooter. He laid there for a few minutes before getting up. I laid on my back, trying to catch my breath.

After we took a shower together, we decided to chill together for the evening. We drank more wine and just chit chatted about every and anything. It was definitely a breath of fresh air and a change from all the drama that was going on.

Loving Him Ain't Worth A Damn Part 2

CHAPTER TWO

Amoy

After crying for days, and trying to get some understanding of everything that went down, I finally managed to get myself together a little so that I could clean up this place. The only reason that I didn't swallow these pills were because of my son. Every time I looked at him, I thanked God for bringing him in my life, but it also saddened me that he was born in all this chaos. He was made out of love, or was he?

I heard my phone ringing. I put the broom down and rushed to the room to get it. I had no idea why I was killing myself to answer the phone when no one called me to see how my son and I were doing. I grabbed the phone and realized that it was Devon. *What the fuck does this bitch ass nigga want?* I thought as I turned around to walk back out of the room. The phone continued ringing back to back. I was getting irritated. I swear I couldn't wait to change my fucking number, so his bum ass could leave me the fuck alone.

"Hello," I said in an aggressive tone.

"You ain't see me calling you?"

"Yeah and? What the fuck you calling me for, fuck nigga?"

"Yo, watch your mouth, B. I know you're pissed off with a nigga, but just hear me out, yo."

Racquel Williams

"Hear you out? I think I heard you loud and clear that day when you were up in my sister's crib in your drawers." I clicked the phone without waiting on a response.

Tears gathered in my eyes. What the fuck did this nigga think he was doing by calling me? He disrespected me in the worst form, and now he was on my fucking phone, trying to talk to me. I threw the fucking phone down on the bed and stormed out of the room.

I went straight to my bathroom and grabbed one of the Percocets that I had gotten for pain but had been popping lately. For some strange reason, it helped me get through this rough time. I washed it down with a can of Sprite that I grabbed out of the fridge. I waited a few minutes, and then the pill started taking its effect, which stabilized my mood. I was feeling more confident now that I was floating. That phone call still had me on the edge. I just prayed that the nigga didn't show his face over here because I would hate to get him locked up.

I finished cleaning up my place. Later on, when my baby woke, I wrapped him up, and we went to the Laundromat to wash some clothes. I'd been slacking lately, and I'd allowed the clothes to pile up on me.

I was standing outside, waiting on a taxi, when the girl, Kaysia, walked by. It had been a minute since I'd seen her. I was hoping the bitch would continue on walking, but I wasn't that lucky.

Loving Him Ain't Worth A Damn Part 2

KENNEDY

It had been days since I had seen or heard from my two-timing ass husband. Truth was, at first, I wasn't too worried 'cause I knew his trifling ass would be back home soon. My husband was used to a woman catering to him, and since I wasn't doing that at the moment, I guess he laid up with one of those ghetto talking bitches.

Ever since I visited the lawyer, I had been thinking hard on what I was going to do. Well, I could just get a divorce and risk his ass getting half of my damn money, or I could - My thoughts were interrupted by the ringing of my telephone. I chuckled as I got up off of the couch and ran to the phone.

"Hey, you." It was Christopher.

"Hey, darling. How are you doing today?"

"I'm feeling much better now that I got to talk with you."

"Is that so? You know exactly what to say to make a woman feel all warm inside."

"Well, that's a good thing. Do you feel like going out to grab a bite?"

"Christopher, just because I gave you the pussy in private doesn't mean we're going to be parading all around town. I'm still a married woman, and I don't want to give that nigga any ammunition to bring to his lawyer."

"I guess you're right. I really enjoy your company, so I guess I got a little above myself. Forgive me, sweet lady."

"No problem, dear. You can stop by tomorrow; I can cook your favorite meal."

"Sounds like a date. Well, let me get back to doing what I do best, following people around."

"Alright, dear."

I knew Christopher's ass was catching feelings, and even though I wished he wasn't, it was a good thing that he was because he could be beneficial to me in the long run.

I heard my phone ringing again. I really hoped it wasn't Christopher again. I looked at the caller ID and realized that it was that cheating ass husband of mine. I thought about not answering it, but I had second thoughts.

"What do you want?"

"Kennedy, I just need to talk to you."

"I have nothing to say to you. Frankly, I wish yo ass was dead somewhere and the fucking crows were feasting on your body parts."

"Damn, yo, that's cold. You're saying this to the man that loves and cares about you."

"Love? How dare you mention you and love in the same sentence? Did you forget all the fucked up shit you did to me? You even went as far as carrying a bastard in this world. Matter-of-fact, I'm done talking to you."

"Kennedy, Kennedy, please don't hang up, babe. I just need you to talk to me face-to-face one time. I promise I just want to talk."

Loving Him Ain't Worth A Damn Part 2

"Ha ha. The last time I saw you, you were chasing after one of those bimbos. What happened to her? She found out you were a fraud, or she ran off with a man with more money than you? Ha ha, my dear husband, it seems like you're shit out of luck."

I didn't wait for a response. Instead, I hung the phone up in his face. The nerve of this man. Who the fuck did he think I was? Some little ass girl that was wet in the ass? I got up off of the bed and walked to the kitchen. I decided to fix a strong drink. One that could numb this pain that I was feeling.

***

I checked the time; it was a little past twelve. I pulled up into the parking lot at the Olive Garden. I was having lunch with the ladies. It had been a minute since we got together like this, and I was looking forward to mingling with them and catching up.

I parked, got out, and walked into the restaurant.

"Yes, may I help you?"

"Kennedy, we're over here," Dorothy said as she waved.

"Yes, hello. I'm with those two ladies."

I walked over to Dorothy, and we hugged and kissed. We walked over to the table where Cecile was sitting.

"Kennedy, my love. Don't you look radiant?" She got up and kissed me on the cheek. We hugged and then took our seats.

"Ladies, it's my pleasure to be here. Wow, it's been a while."

"Uh huh, it's only been a while because you fell head over heels over that young hunk and threw us to the side. By the way, how is married life treating you?"

"Married life is just fine. Everything is just fine," I lied.

"Are you sure because I heard from a close friend of ours that he was parading around town with a younger woman. She said he looked shocked when she asked about you."

"Dorothy, I said everything is just fine. Now drop it."

"I'm sorry, Kennedy. I just want you to know we are here for you if you need us. We women have to stick together."

"Hello, ladies. Are y'all ready to order?" The waitress interrupted us. I was happy she did because I wasn't feeling this conversation. Maybe it was because I was living a damn lie, and I was too embarrassed.

After our meal came, we ate, laughed, and fooled around, just like old times. It really felt good to be out and not worrying about all of the chaos that was taking place in my life.

"Okay, ladies, we need to do this again soon." I hugged them both and walked off to my car. As I pulled off, I couldn't help but think about what Dorothy said about my husband. See, this shit angered me; it was one thing to be slinging that dick in private, but it was a whole different level of disrespect when he was out and about with his whores, knowing damn well I was well known in this damn county.

Loving Him Ain't Worth A Damn Part 2

After I got home, I took out a pack of oxtails. Even though my nerves were bad and I had already ate, I remembered that I promised Christopher I was going to cook for him. I was a woman of my word, so I put my feelings to the side and threw down in the kitchen.

After I finished cooking, I took a shower and decided to lay down for a few. I was feeling drained and needed a quick nap before he got here.

"You are gonna pay for what you did to me; I promise that. You have everyone around here fooled, like you're this grieving widow, but sooner or later, you will be exposed for the fraud that you are…"

"Travis, is that you?" I jumped up and looked around. I didn't see anyone. That was when it hit me that I was sleeping, and I had a dream about Travis, my late husband. What the hell did that mean? This was the first time since he died that I had a dream about him. It seemed so real as I replayed the cold words he said to me.

I got up off of the bed and rushed to the bathroom. I brushed my teeth and washed my face. "Travis, you devil, I wasn't scared of you when you were alive, and I damn sure ain't scared of your ghost. You better go to hell before I kill yo ass again." I wiped my face and put on some cocoa butter.

I wasn't going to lie. That shit scared the hell out of me. He had been dead for years; why did he feel the need to pop up in my dreams now? Was he trying to send me a sign or something? Hmmm, all kinds of crazy thoughts ran through my mind. I made a mental note to call the lead detective that was handling my husband's case. It had been a minute since we spoke.

I walked in the kitchen and poured a glass of gin. I wasted no time in swallowing the hot liquor. I cringed as it burned my chest, but I continued drinking. "Kennedy, it's nothing. Calm down," I said to myself.

I heard the doorbell ringing, and I jumped. That was when I remembered that Christopher was coming over for dinner. After that dream that I had, I really didn't feel like entertaining, but the food was finished, and my guest was here, so there was no use in cancelling on him.

"Hello there, gorgeous," he said and walked into the house.

"Hello there. I fell asleep, so I need to warm up the food. Do you want something to drink?"

"What you got there?"

"Hmmm. Let's see. I've got gin, vodka, wine, and I have a few beers."

"Let me get vodka on the rocks."

"Coming right up."

After I made his drink, I walked in the kitchen to warm the food. I was tending to the oxtails on the stove when I felt someone breathing down my back. I jumped again, but he grabbed me. "I didn't mean to scare you. You seem a little frightened. Are you okay?"

"Yes, just making sure I don't burn the oxtails."

Loving Him Ain't Worth A Damn Part 2

He held me, and I swear it felt kind of good. My nerves were all over the place, and the alcohol helped to calm me down a little but not all the way.

He started kissing my neck while massaging my breast. "You better stop before you start something that you can't finish," I teased, pretending like I didn't like it, but honestly, I loved it.

"Go sit down, so I can dish this food out," I demanded.

"Yes, ma'am." He kissed me on the back of my neck before he walked off.

I brought the plates to the table. I sat across from him while he blessed the food. I was about to start eating when the loud ding from the doorbell startled me. Christopher looked over at me.

"Are you expecting a visitor?"

"Not that I know of."

I got up from the table and walked towards the door. Before I could ask who it was, the person sat on the doorbell, just ringing it.

"Who the hell is it?" I said as I popped the door wide open.

"Hello, wife. It's your husband." Devon stood there, laughing, like he was a fucking fool.

"What are you doing here? I told you I have nothing to say to you."

"Whose car is that in the driveway?"

"None of your damn business. Now go on."

Racquel Williams

"I'm not going anywhere. Whose car is it, Kennedy? What? You got another nigga up in our house? You're cheating?" He bombarded me with questions.

Before I could respond, he pushed past me, flinging the door wider, and almost knocked me to the ground.

"Who is in here, Kennedy? Come on out, nigga."

I saw when Christopher stood up and walked towards Devon.

"Yo, my nigga, what the fuck you doing up in here? Do you know this is my house and my bitch?"

"The lady of the house invited me over, and you might want to watch your mouth. This is a queen, not a female dog."

"Nigga, fuck all that you're talking. Old Malcolm X ass nigga. This is my bitch and my house, which mean you're trespassing."

"You need to stop now! Christopher is my good friend, and we're having dinner. Matter-of-fact, you shouldn't be here. You don't live here anymore."

"I ain't going anywhere. I know the law; you can't just put me out, wife," he said sarcastically.

"Kennedy, what do you want to do? Do you want me to put this fool out?" Christopher asked in a very serious tone.

I knew then that things could really get serious up in here.

"Christopher, you know what? I'm sorry that you had to encounter this. Go ahead and go home."

Loving Him Ain't Worth A Damn Part 2

"Yes, pussy nigga. Go ahead and go home. This is my bitch, so stay the fuck away from her. You heard?"

"Ha ha, you're a young, silly nigga. You're lucky the lady didn't give me the word to body your ass right here on her floor. See you around." Christopher winked at him before he walked through the door.

"Fuck you, nigga," Devon yelled, but Christopher was long gone.

"What the fuck you call yourself doing?" I turned to face this bastard.

"You fucking that nigga?"

"Matter-of-fact, I am. You think you can be out here, running around and slinging that dick all over town, and I'm supposed to sit in here, lonely and shit? Wrong. I have needs, and he satisfies them."

"Really, Kennedy? I should fucking smack the fuck out of you right now. How dare you bring another nigga up in our house? Our bed?"

"Darling, this is my pussy, my got damn house, and my bed. You came in this marriage with the clothes on your back, and you will leave with just that, the clothes on your back."

"I already told your ass I ain't going nowhere. So, you better call that fuck nigga and let him know that whatever y'all had going on is over."

Racquel Williams

"You're a fucking joke. I will get you out of my house, one way or another," I said before I stormed to my bedroom and locked my door.

It was time to put my plan into action.

Loving Him Ain't Worth A Damn Part 2

CHAPTER THREE

Amoy

It was Friday night, and I was bored out of my damn mind. I remembered the days when I was free and could hang out and do what I wanted to do. Not these days. All I had was my baby boy and myself. It wasn't all bad though because I loved spending time with him and welcomed the way he made me feel.

I was lying on the couch, catching up on an episode of *Deadly Wives* on the ID channel. I heard my cell phone ringing, so I picked it up. It was Marquise. I rolled my eyes, wondering what the hell he wanted. I had not heard from him since the day that shit popped off between him and Devon.

"Hey, stranger."

"Aye, yo, what's good, ma?"

"Nothing. I didn't know you remembered my number," I said sarcastically.

"Girl, chill out wit' all that. Is that chump over there?"

"Ain't nobody over here but me and my baby."

"That's good cause I'm about to pass through in a minute."

"Okay."

I didn't ask him why or anything. I mean, I still loved him, even though we hadn't fucked with each other in a minute. Sometimes, I wished that I hadn't fucked up with him, but guess what? There was no need for me to cry over spilled milk.

Racquel Williams

I must have dozed off because I heard a loud banging at the door. It was so loud that it scared the hell out of me. I got up, cut the light on, and walked over to the door. I saw that it was Marquise, so I opened the door.

"Yo, what's good?" He walked inside.

I locked the door behind us, and he walked over to me. "Damn, can a nigga get a hug?"

"Of course. You know you can."

"That's what I'm talking about." He laughed and pulled me closer to him.

His masculine smell leaked through his pores, hitting my nose. I tried to ease out of his grip, but he pulled me in closer and gripped my butt cheeks with his hands. Part of me wanted to pull away, but the other part welcomed this little bit of attention that I was getting.

After we finished hugging, he walked over to the couch and sat down. "Where's little man at?"

"Taking a nap. He ran me ragged today. Shit, my ass was sleeping before you called."

"Damn... That's what I came over here for. I want to talk to you."

"About what?" He had my full attention.

"Do you think lil' man is really mine?"

I sat there, quiet for a few minutes, thinking of ways to put my words together without coming off as a slut.

Loving Him Ain't Worth A Damn Part 2

"To be honest, Marquise, I really don't know whose child he is. I slept with you right before I slept with old boy. I didn't know I was pregnant until a few weeks after."

"Damn, B. I ain't never consider you to be that kind…"

"That kind of what?" I cut him off and stared him down with an attitude.

"Nah, ma. I ain't mean no disrespect to you, but it's kind of careless that you're fucking niggas without protection. You dig?"

"You're acting like I ran around here, just fucking random niggas without condoms. Before you start judging me, make sure your shit is clean for real. If I can remember right, you were the one slinging dick around here."

"Amoy, I understand you're upset at what I just said, but this ain't about me for real."

The tears welled up in my eyes. I couldn't believe this nigga was coming at me like that. I should've kept my mouth shut.

"Man, don't do that. You know damn well I didn't mean no harm by what I just said. We're supposed to be able to talk to each other about how we're feeling. I mean, when I first found out you were pregnant, I asked you if he was mine. You blurted out no, only for you to tell me after he was born that there was a possibility that he was mine. I mean, that shit bothered the fuck outta me. I ain't got no other seed out there, and if he's mine, I want to be in his life. I ain't never had no pops, so I know what it's like to be out here without one." He choked up.

"I'm sorry if I hurt you. I just don't know who his father is, and I didn't know how to tell you."

"So, did you tell that other nigga he might not be the daddy, or are you still letting him think he's the daddy?"

"I had told my sister, and she told him the other day. I found out him and my sister have been fucking around, so I don't fuck with him anymore. Plus, we have a case going on."

"What kind of case?"

"Him putting his hands on me."

"What the fuck, yo? What happened to the burner I gave you? You letting niggas put their hands on you and shit. Man, you need to boss up real fast."

I wasn't proud to tell him this, and the way he was reacting, I probably should've kept it to myself.

"Listen, Marquise, I never pretended like I was perfect. Shit, my life's been pure hell since the day I was born, but I'm not sitting around moping. I'll admit it; I made some bad decisions, and I'm trying my best to clean them up, but it's not easy."

He reached over and wrapped his arms around me. I laid my head on his shoulder and let it all out.

"Yo, e'erything goin' be aiight. I promise you that, B. I mean, you deserve so much more than this bullshit for real. I know I didn't make it no better when I cheated on you over and over. I wish I didn't, but it is what it is."

I heard his words loud and clear, but I didn't know what to believe anymore. I had a feeling that I was never going to experience happiness.

***

I opened my eyes and stretched my arms out. My hand bumped into something, and that was when it hit me. I was not in my bed alone. Last night, after our long talk, we started drinking and smoking. I remembered that we started kissing. I dragged my memory to see what else I remembered.

I looked down; I was butt ass naked. I looked over at him; his ass was naked also. I knew then that we got it in, and I was tired as hell. I just prayed to God that he didn't cum in me 'cause I wasn't on the pill and I wasn't ready to have another baby this soon. I was already struggling with raising one.

I jumped out the bed and reached for my robe that was hanging on the closet door. First, I went to check on little man. He seemed to be just getting up.

"Good morning, Mommy's Pooh," I said as I picked him up. I kissed him on the forehead. After I changed him, I made him a bottle and put him in his playpen. I washed my face and put on a pair of panties.

Racquel Williams

I sat in the living room, watching my baby and thinking about what went down last night. Lord, I still had feelings for that boy, but I also remembered the reasons why I left him alone. He was a real nigga that made sure I had everything that I needed, but his ass couldn't keep his dick in his pants. I had busted a few of these bitches in the head over this nigga. After a while, the shit got old, and I decided that, even though I loved him, I deserved better.

Lord, now here I was, waking up with this nigga in my bed. My feelings were all over the place, feelings that I'd buried deep inside.

"Yo, why you ain't wake me up?" he said as he walked up on me.

"Oh my bad. You were sleeping so peacefully that I didn't want to disturb you."

"Nah, I 'ont usually sleep this late. You know a nigga's got to be out here in these streets."

"Yeah," was all I whispered.

I was feeling all kinds of emotions. Maybe it was a mistake giving him the pussy because now I wanted to pour my soul out to him.

"Yo, B, you aiight?"

"Hey there, little man." He walked over to the playpen and gently took my son out.

I watched as he examined him while he pretended like he was only playing with him.

"He kind of resembles me. What you think?"

Loving Him Ain't Worth A Damn Part 2

I looked at both of them side by side. I did see the resemblance, but I was cautious. I didn't want him to get all attached and then the test came back and he wasn't the father.

He sat him down on the carpet and started playing with him. This was the first time a man really took the time out to pay attention to my son. Devon's ass never gave him the time of day. Tears welled up in my eyes as emotions took over. I was really wishing he was the father because, even though he had whorish ways, I still believed he would be a great father. "God, please let him be the father," I whispered under my breath.

After he finished playing with Jamal, he placed him back in the playpen, and then he stood up.

"Listen, B, I've got some business to go handle. I'ma hit you up later. Do you need anything before I go?"

"Nah, I'm straight," I lied.

I could definitely use a few dollars, but I wasn't going to be desperate.

"Aiight, I'ma holla at y'all."

He unlocked the door and left out. I stood by the door for a minute. I felt like a part of me had just left. I knew I was tripping. Just because we fucked didn't mean we were getting back together. I tried to put him out of my mind because I didn't want to get disappointed.

Racquel Williams

SHARI

I left the house early to go register for school. Yes, a bitch was sexy and bougie, but I needed an education to back that shit up. See, I wasn't no regular bitch, and my plan, ever since I was young, was to become a massage therapist. After I finished filling out the paperwork and went to see financial aid, I headed back to Mount Vernon.

Earlier, when I left, Devon was still asleep. I was going to wake him up because the nigga needed a damn job or his ass needed to get out there and sling some rocks. Every day, I had to listen to him brag about how he was the nigga in the streets, but he changed. I didn't know what kind of bitch he thought I was, but if a nigga didn't have any money, I damn sure wasn't fucking with him. This pussy was too damn good to be throwing it away on broke, useless niggas.

I pulled up at the house and realized his car wasn't there. *Well, I hope his ass is out getting some money,* I thought as I parked.

I got out of the car and grabbed my stuff. I walked up the stairs and opened my door. The stench of old food hit my nose. Damn, this nigga couldn't even take out the garbage. That shit gave me an instant attitude. It got even worse when I entered the kitchen and saw that he cooked and left all the plates in the sink for the fucking maid to wash. I was furious at this dude. I grabbed my cellphone out of my purse and called him. The phone just rang out. I hit redial, and the same thing happened again. This was very strange. Not one time since we'd been fucking with each other had I called him and he didn't pick up.

Loving Him Ain't Worth A Damn Part 2

Maybe I was getting worked up for nothing. He did tell me he was going to be back out in the streets. I figured he was caught up, handling business. I calmed myself down a little bit.

I ended up ordering some wings and pizza for dinner. I rolled a blunt and grabbed a beer out of the fridge. This shit was nasty as fuck, but it was the only thing to drink, and I didn't feel like running out to the store right now. I grabbed my phone and hit Devon's phone again; this time, the phone went straight to voicemail. This time, I was angrier than before because it was well past 11 P.M., and I hadn't heard from this nigga all day. I thought about calling the jails and the hospitals but decided against it. That nigga knew my fucking number and never had a problem using it before. What the fuck did he think? I was going to be up and chasing behind his ass?

After drinking about three beers, and smoking the blunt, I started feeling horny. Shit, I wished he was home to give me the dick, but he wasn't, so his loss. I scanned through my contact list to see who the fuck was available to come through. I stopped on the nigga, DJ's name. He was a big time stick up kid from the Bronx. We went to Evander Childs High School together, and we fucked a few times. I stopped fucking around with him 'cause that nigga was living recklessly, getting chased by the police a few times and had niggas shooting up his car and shit. I was too damn cute to be dead in somebody's morgue. My past memories of him didn't stop me from calling his number though.

41

I laid on my back, playing with my pussy while the phone rang.

"Yoooo," he answered.

"Hey, babes. How you doing?"

"Damn, B, you know you were on my mind the other day."

"I hope it was the good fuck that I gave you the last time that you're thinking about," I said sexually.

"You know you got that sugar pussy, babes. So, what's good though?"

"I was just feeling horny, so I'm trying to see if you want to slide through."

"Damn, bae. You know a nigga can't turn down no good pussy. Text me your address. I'll slide through real quick and beat up the pussy for you real quick."

"Aiight, boo. I'll see you in a few."

After I hung the phone up, I texted him the address. I knew I was being reckless by inviting him over here, but this was my shit, and I didn't give a fuck for real. I went to take a quick shower, so I could freshen up the pussy before he got here.

I laid on my bed, waiting on him to come through. I decided to jump on Facebook to see what was going on. All these niggas and bitches did was lie and fake, trying to impress bitches and other niggas. There was no drama going on on my timeline. I put my sister's name in; I was about to see what was going on on her page.

'Add Friend'.

Loving Him Ain't Worth A Damn Part 2

So this silly bitch unfriended me? Wow, she must have thought that I was going to roll over and die because she didn't want to be friends on social media. Bitch, I didn't give a fuck that we were family. I still took your whole man and didn't give a fuck.

I should send that hoe a request, just to be funny, I thought.

That thought was interrupted when I heard my doorbell ringing. It could be Devon or it could be DJ. I hoped it was DJ. I was trying to fuck. I walked over and peeped out. I saw that it was DJ. I quickly opened the door and let him in.

"What's good, baby girl?"

"Just here, trying to live," I said as I sashayed to the living room.

"Damn, B, that ass got fatter than the last time that I saw you."

"Really? The pussy got wetter too. Come on; let me show you."

By the time he got to where I was, I was already butt ass naked. DJ was a freaky ass nigga, and I was a nasty ass female, so together, we knew exactly what we wanted. I wasted no time; I dropped to my knees, taking all that big, black dick into my mouth. I slobbed all over it and then slowly licked it off. He grabbed the back of my head and brought it closer to his dick. I started deep throating it; it felt very good when I felt it touching the back of my throat. Some bitches often gagged doing this technique, but I was a bad bitch, and I'd built my tolerance up.

He fucked my throat for a good ten minutes, and then he exploded in my mouth. I didn't move an inch; I swallowed every drop of his protein shake and then used my tongue to lick up the remaining milk.

"Come here, B." He pulled me up. He took a seat on the couch and pulled me on top of him.

"Ride this dick, yo," he commanded.

He didn't have to tell me twice. I parted my legs apart and slid down on his already hard dick. This nigga was definitely blessed with size, but I still tried my best to maneuver. After my pussy got super wet, the dick slipped all the way in. I placed my hand on his shoulder, stuck my butt out, and rode that dick like I was a porn star.

"Damn, B… Take your time. You tryna break a nigga's dick head off?"

"Nah, babe. This dick is just so fucking good. You have no idea. Aweee," I moaned out.

The dick was good, but that wasn't the reason why I was bouncing that hard on it. I was taking all my frustrations out on the dick. My mind was all over the place, wondering where the fuck Devon was and why he was not here.

"Damn, B, I'm about to cum. Are you on the pill?" he said as he pulled me down and gripped me tightly.

"Stop. Let me up, yo. I ain't on no damn pill," I said as I tried to get out of his grip.

Loving Him Ain't Worth A Damn Part 2

Seconds later, his juice squirted out, all up in my pussy. He then let me up, and I jumped off.

"What the fuck did you do that for? I ain't tryna have no damn baby." I lashed out in an aggressive tone.

"Chill out, yo. My sperm count is low 'cause of all this weed I smoke. I can't make no damn baby."

"Boy, shut the fuck up. That shit is a lie that niggas make up."

"Nah, I'm for real. But just in case something did go wrong, hit me up. I've got the abortion money."

"You better 'cause I'm not ready to be no damn mommy."

To be honest, it wasn't that I wasn't ready to be a mother; I just didn't want to have a baby by him.

After we finished fucking, we ended up taking a shower and fucked again. This time, he did pull out. After we were finished, we got out and got dressed.

I was drained as hell, so I flopped down on the couch. "You good, B?"

"Yeah, you done wore my ass out."

"Shit, ain't that what you wanted? For me to come over here and beat the pussy up?"

"Ha ha, you right."

"Aiight, yo, I've got to bounce. Hit me up when you need me to slide through again."

"Okay, cool."

I sat there as he opened the door and left out. I was drained and couldn't move at the moment.

***

I jumped out of my sleep. I looked around and realized that I was still on the couch. I was that tired last night that my ass didn't move a muscle. I searched around for my phone. I didn't see it, so I got up and walked to the bedroom. It was still on the charger from last night. I grabbed it, hoping to see a ton of missed calls or texts from Devon. To my disappointment, there were no missed calls or texts from him. Not one got damn phone call. This was getting serious. I ran over to the closet, where he kept his clothes at, and everything was still there. I stood there, scratching my head, trying to figure out what the fuck was going on.

I called his phone again, and there was still no answer, so I shot him a message.

Hey, not sure what's going on, but I have not heard from you since yesterday... Please let me know something.

I waited a few minutes, to see if I would get a text back, but nothing came through. I started feeling desperate. This was the reason why I didn't fall in love with niggas. I didn't like this desperate feeling. I searched through my phone, where I had his wife's number programmed. I didn't give a fuck; I needed to know what was going on.

The phone started ringing, and I thought about hanging up.

Loving Him Ain't Worth A Damn Part 2

"Hello," the old bitch answered.

"Good morning. Can I speak to Devon?"

"Hmmm. May I ask who this is?"

"Listen, bitch, does it matter who it is? Is he there?"

"Little girl, get your filthy ass off my phone. You're calling my phone, looking for my husband, so I assume he done slung a little dick your way, and now you can't find him. Next time you decide to give up your pussy so freely, you may want to make sure he doesn't belong to another woman."

I was ready to roast this bitch, but she hung up in my face. I tried calling back, but she didn't pick up. "Aargh, you scary bitch," I yelled out.

I still didn't get the answer I needed. *Where the fuck are you, Devon?* I decided to get dressed and leave out. I was so angry that my vision was blurred. The honking of a horn from a big rig truck caught my attention. I swerved to the side in order to prevent running into the truck's path. After I swerved, I sort of regretted it. I should've just let the truck hit me and end it all. Who was going to miss me? No fucking body. Well, maybe Mama, but that bitch might be so high that she probably wouldn't realize that I was gone.

I continued driving. This time, I tried to stay focused. I pulled up at my sister's apartment complex. I pulled up two spaces down and glanced around. I didn't see his car. I noticed her car in her parking space. I circled around twice to make sure I didn't miss anything. I was convinced that he wasn't there, so I pulled off.

I tried racking my brain to where he might be, but nothing came to mind.

Loving Him Ain't Worth A Damn Part 2

KENNEDY

"Lord, please bless this little hoe that called my phone this morning because she knows not what she has done. In Jesus name, I pray." I got up off of my knees.

I walked over to the guest room, where this bum was staying, and knocked.

"Come in," he yelled out.

I busted the door open. He was lying on top of his cover, butt ass naked, with his dick hard as hell. It seemed like the nigga was beating off.

"I'm going to tell you this one damn time. Get your little hoes under wrap and don't let them call my damn phone, looking for you, again."

He threw the covers over himself and sat up in the bed.

"Man, what the fuck you talkin' 'bout? It's too early for you to be here, bitching and shit. C'mon, man, can a nigga breathe a little?"

"You know what, Devon? The more I fucking see what kind of joke you really are, the more I despise yo sorry ass. Oh, and by the way, I heard one of the ladies bumped into you while you were parading your little bitch around town. How low would you stoop, trying to embarrass me?"

"That bitch is lying. Ain't nobody see me doing shit wit' no bitch. I told you from day one that them bitches are mad that you have a man in your life and they ain't got nobody to fuck them."

49

"You sound silly as hell if you think I would believe shit that's coming out of your mouth. You better clear that shit up before I snap on you and them hoes. I don't think either of y'all know what deadly game y'all are playing. Trust me, I don't pay fair."

I shot his ass an evil look and rushed out of the room. This couldn't be the man that I fell for. Shit, he didn't even look the same. It looked like he was famished and on some kind of drugs.

I walked back into my room and dialed Christopher's number.

"Good morning, beautiful," his raspy voice echoed.

"Good morning, Christopher. I need to send you a number; I need a name to go with it."

"Oh, Lord, who's in trouble now?" he chuckled.

"Hmmm, a young slut that has no business calling my phone."

"Well, my dear, I will have that info for you in a few."

"Aiight, dear."

I hung up feeling pleased. As soon as Christopher got back with me, I'd be paying that rude bitch a visit.

Loving Him Ain't Worth A Damn Part 2

CHAPTER FOUR

Amoy

Marquise was over, visiting us again. His visits were more frequent, and he had been buying groceries, pampers, and wipes, and he had even bought my baby two pairs of Jordan's. I kept reminding him that, since he wasn't sure that he was the father, to stop buying all of these things. He didn't listen to me because, every time he walked through the door, he had bags in his hands.

They were both still asleep when I decided to sneak out of the room and make some breakfast. I quickly tidied up the living room and started cooking. I had the music turned down, but it was loud enough for me to hear it. I was definitely jamming this morning to Pandora. I didn't know what we were doing; I just knew that I was loving it.

"Good morning, beautiful." He kissed me on my neck, scaring the hell out of me. I jumped.

"Good morning." I wasn't too sure what to call him.

"Damn, that's what I'm talking about. Baby girl's up, making her daddy breakfast."

He slid his hands up under my nightgown, caressing my breasts. It was something about this nigga's hands that did something to me.

"Boy, stop playing before you make me burn these darn pancakes." I giggled but was enjoying the way he massaged my breasts.

"Man, fuck them pancakes. I'm trying to get in them drawers real quick."

He took the fork out of my hand, took two pancakes out of the frying pan, and cut the stove off. He picked me up and placed me on the countertop. He took my nightgown over my head, leaving me naked. I was already wet, and my pussy was yearning for his dick. He pulled me down, towards him, and slid up in me.

"Awee." I gasped as he ripped through my love hole.

"Damn, this pussy's wet and tight, ma," he whispered in my ear as he dug deeper and deeper in.

I hugged him and braced myself for the pain that came along with getting fucked good.

"Awee, baby, I love you. Please fuck me; please fuck me," I pleaded with him.

He heard my cries because he parted my legs and threw the dick on me. I started shaking. I sunk my fingers deep in his back and yelled out, "Yes, Daddy. Fuck meeee." I then exploded all over his dick. He continued throwing the dick until his veins started getting bigger. I knew then that he was about to bust. "Please pull out," I said as I continued twerking on his dick.

"Nah, you good."

I didn't have time to ask him what he meant; his juice exploded all up in me. I jumped down, and the juice ran down my leg. I ran to the bathroom to take a quick shower. "God, why did I let this nigga cum up in me?" I whispered.

After I finished bathing, I got out and quickly got dressed. I walked in the kitchen; he was in there, finishing up breakfast. I smiled at him and just walked off to go check on my baby. I stood over my son's bed, just looking at him. I really wished this was his father because this could be my little family. I let out a long sigh and walked back out of the room. Before I walked back into the kitchen, I heard him on his phone.

"Yo, I told you I'ma come through in a little while," he said.

"Aiight, man, I'm gone."

He hung the phone up, and I walked into the kitchen. I grabbed one of my son's bottles, so I could make him some formula with cereal.

"You aiight?"

"Yeah, I'm good."

"You ain't get in trouble wit' your chick, right?" I quizzed.

"Man, cut it out. I ain't got no damn girl," he said with an attitude.

I decided to drop it because, clearly, I could see that he was bothered by that phone call.

After he finished cooking pancakes, eggs, and sausage, we sat at the table, eating. I was kind of feeling some type of way about how he spoke to me a few minutes ago. I took a sip of my orange juice.

He reached over and snatched my arm. "Aye, listen, I'm sorry for snapping a little while ago, man."

"It's cool. I was out of line," I lied.

"Man, cut it out, yo. I know when you're bothered."

"Why should I be bothered? It ain't like you're my nigga or we on some serious shit."

"So you ain't tryna fuck wit' a nigga?"

"You ain't say anything about us getting back together."

"Yo, B, I've always loved you. One night, I was out and about. I was high and drunk, and I was in my feelings. I asked God what was I doing wrong and why couldn't I find a good woman. I mean, I make good money, but what's that if I don't have no one to enjoy life with? I was searching for answers; that's when it hit me that she was right in front of me all along."

I looked at him. "Hmm, who you talking about?"

"You silly. From the day that we met, I knew you were my soulmate, but I was young and stupid and was still into trying to fuck a lot of bitches."

I sat there, listening to what he was saying. Why had I heard this statement before? I knew niggas said the darnest things when they were trying to convince women that they were worth a try. Part of me believed him, but the other part remembered all the shit that I went through with that asshole. I was still hurting inside, even though I tried to hide it. I knew, mentally, I wasn't ready for another relationship this fast when I still had unfinished emotions floating around.

"You know I've always loved you, but I remember how you used to cheat and lie to cover it up. How I used to call your phone and you would ignore me. You hurt me badly. How do I know this time is different?"

"You don't know… All I've got is my word, ma. I can only show you from this day on that I'm one hunnit wit' you if you give our love another chance."

"Are you here because of love or is it because you think Jamal might be your son?" I looked him dead in the eyes.

"I'm here because of you. Yeah, I'm hoping he's mine, but for real, B, even if the test turns out that he's that fuck nigga's seed, I still want to be with you. I want a family with you. I'm tired of these streets, and I plan on getting out in a year's time."

I wanted to say that this was all bullshit he was spitting, but I saw the sincerity in his eyes. Behind all that hardness I saw the good part of him. And it was that same moment that I fell back in love with him.

The loud crying of my baby interrupted our little heart to heart talk. "I think someone feels left out," he said.

We both burst out laughing. I got up from the table and went to his room.

"Hey, Mommy's Pooh." I picked him up.

As I changed his diaper, I took an extra look at his features. To be honest, I couldn't call it one way or the other. I could only pray for it to work out in our favor.

***

An hour later, Marquise left, and it was back to being lil man and I. I cut on kids' cartoons for him while I grabbed my computer. I decided that it was time for me to get back in the work field. Money was tight after that asshole stopped giving money to us, and I got a letter that rent was due. I guess his ass stopped paying that also. I knew that, if I asked Marquise, he would help me, but I preferred to figure it out for myself. I didn't want to start depending on niggas too much after all that I'd been through. I was responsible for providing for me and my little man. I also looked up beauty school. I was a beast at braiding hair, but I really wanted a license so I could do more than that, possibly open my own shop one day.

I heard my cell phone ringing, so I grabbed it up without looking at the caller ID. "Hello."

"Is Devon over there?"

I removed the phone from my ear to look at the number. I was correct; it was my slut ass sister on my damn phone.

"Bitch, are you crazy? Don't you ever call my phone, asking for that bum ass nigga. Ha ha, he must be over the next bitch's house. You might want to call her number," I said sarcastically and hung my phone up.

Loving Him Ain't Worth A Damn Part 2

The nerves of that hoe. I swear that little bitch knocked her head when she was a baby because she wasn't wrapped too damn tight. What the fuck she thought? He was going to leave me for her and then be faithful to her? That bum had a whole wife.

Oh, Lord. I shook that negative energy off and went back to what I was doing before this stupid ass bitch interrupted me. As a matter-of-fact, I grabbed my phone back up and pulled her number up. I went ahead and blocked that ass. It saddened me that I had to do that, but that bitch was disrespectful and was dead, just like her fucking mama was to me.

After I finished filling out applications, I pulled up information on how to get a paternity test done. I'd been putting it off for long enough.

Racquel Williams

SHARI

I swear I felt like I was losing my mind. *What the fuck did I do to his ass for him to carry it this raw with me?* I asked myself as I took several pulls off of the weed that I copped earlier. I had called the bitch that he was married to and the bitch that he supposedly had a baby with, and both of these bitches carried it. I knew what it was; their asses were just jealous 'cause he didn't want them. But wait, if he wasn't with them, where the fuck was he? Was he with another bitch that I wasn't aware of? I had too many damn questions and no damn answers. It had been three days, and I hadn't received not one text or phone call. I really thought him and I were on the same page, but I guess not. I took several more pulls and started coughing. "Damn, bitch, take yo time," I said out loud to myself.

I heard my phone ringing, and I jumped to pick it up. I accidentally dropped the blunt. *Fuck,* I thought as I picked it up hurriedly before it burned my couch. Shit, I had to fuck a nigga a few times to get the money to buy my living room suite. By the time I got to the phone, it had stopped ringing. It was Mama's number. I was disappointed because I was really praying it was Devon. I flopped back down on the couch. *Man, what the fuck this lady want right now?*

I dialed back her number. I laid on my back, staring up at the ceiling.

"Yeah."

"Hey, baby. Why you ain't pick up the phone?"

Loving Him Ain't Worth A Damn Part 2

"Ma, it don't matter why I ain't pick up. I called you back, right?" I was annoyed, not really with her, but with what I was dealing with.

"Damn, who pissed you off? This wouldn't have nothing to do with that boy?"

"Ma, what boy are you talking about?" I was ready to hang up on her ass for real.

"The boy that your sister said you took from her."

"When the fuck she told you this?"

"Watch yo got damn mouth... You done lost your mind."

"Ma, I'm grown as hell, and in case you haven't noticed, I have my own place, so I can cuss as much as I want to."

"Mmm hmm, you still my damn baby."

"Ma, when did she tell you that?"

"Girl, I don't know. One day, she popped up over here, talking 'bout I was in on it. I cussed her little pissy ass out. She knows better than to put me in some shit. Your pussy is yours, and you're free to screw whoever you want."

"That chick's funny. If he was hers, I couldn't take him. Anyway, she needs to go find out who her real baby daddy is."

"Say what? That boy not her baby daddy?"

"Nah, you know yo daughter a hoe. She better keep my motherfucking name out of her mouth before I run up on that ass."

"Hmm, well, I just want to know if you had a few dollars to spare?"

"I knew that was the only reason why you called me. Where is that nigga at that you have laid up over there? He does know ain't nothing free in this world, not even pussy."

"He 'ont get paid until Friday, and I just need a few dollars to keep me over until then."

"So you can buy drugs?"

"Shari, come on now. I ain't got nothing to smoke in a while. Your mama is trying to clean up her life. Watch, you goin' be proud of your mama."

"Listen, I've got to go. Come by later and get it."

"Alright, baby. Mama loves you."

I hung the phone up without responding. I swear I loved my mama to death. I just wished she would leave that nigga and the drugs alone. I told her numerous times that I would help her get into rehab, and a few times, she agreed until that nigga got into her ear, thinking she could go cold turkey. If you asked me, his nasty ass loved keeping her high so she could depend on him.

***

I must've dozed off because banging on the door woke me up. I jumped up and ran to the door.

"Damn, Ma, why the fuck you banging on my door like you're the police?"

"Sorry, baby, but I was calling you to let you know I was on the way, but you didn't pick up."

Loving Him Ain't Worth A Damn Part 2

"Maybe 'cause my ass was sleeping."

I walked off to grab my purse. I shouldn't have told her I was going to give her shit. I grabbed forty dollars out of my purse. I walked back into the living room. I saw her all up in my fridge, looking around.

"Why you up in my shit?"

"I'm hungry as hell, but it looks like you ain't been to the store lately."

"Close my fridge. Here goes forty dollars. Please spend it wisely 'cause I ain't got no more to spare."

She snatched the money out of my hand, and her eyes lit up.

"God bless you, baby. Mama loves you."

She walked through the door, and I locked it. I walked over to the window and saw as she got into a car and handed the money to a man that was driving. I closed my curtains and shook my head.

I was tired of sitting around here, hoping this nigga would show up. I needed to get back out there and start playing these niggas for their money. I really didn't know what in the hell had gotten into me with this nigga because I had never been so gone over no dick. Shit, to be honest, I kind of loved pussy more than dick. Maybe I needed to get back on that shit. That was when Kaysia ran through my mind. I still couldn't believe that bitch snitched on me to my sister. Old jealous ass hoe...

Racquel Williams

I was definitely starving, and Mama was right. A bitch hadn't been to the grocery store in days. I decided to order some Chinese food. That little place over on Sanford Boulevard's food was off the chain. After I placed the order, I decided to take a quick shower before they came.

I was feeling horny as fuck, so while the water beat my skin, I started to play with my pussy. I felt so good fucking myself that I started working my fingers harder, and I grinded my pussy down on my fingers.

"Awe, baby, damn this feels so good," I moaned out as I started going faster. My temperature rose, and I started getting hot. "Oh, shit, aweee, oweiiii." I exploded all over my fingers. I got lightheaded, so I held on to the wall for support. Even though I was weak, that shit felt damn good. I put my fingers between my legs and then licked it off.

"Shit, bitch, you taste damn good too," I said out loud as I resumed washing myself off.

As soon as I got out of the tub, I heard a loud banging on the door. *Who the fuck is that?* I thought.

I wrapped the towel around me and walked to the door. The knocking was getting louder, and I was ready to curse out whoever it was. "Who is it?" I yelled.

"It's Devon," he yelled.

My heart skipped a few beats. I didn't know what I wanted to do. Did I want to let him in or just not answer the door? Truth was, I was happy to see him, and even though he had made me mad, I was weak for him.

"Yeah, what do you want?" I opened the door and asked him.

"What the fuck you doing, coming to the door in just a towel? What, you got a nigga up in here?" He pushed past me and started looking around.

I locked the door and stood there, looking at this mad man walking through the house, looking in closets and under the bed.

"For a nigga that's been gone for more than a week, you've got some fucking nerves coming up in here, acting like you run shit."

"Yo, what the fuck is that s'ppose to mean? What? You got another nigga now?"

"You know what, Devon? You're fucking ridiculous. You know you're in the wrong, so you run up in here, acting like you own me. Nah, nigga, the minute you pulled that little disappearing act, this pussy was up for gra..."

Before I could finish my sentence, this nigga lunged forward and grabbed my neck with one hand, forcing me up into the wall.

"Bitch, you better not play with me. Yo, you just don't know, B." He squeezed my neck.

"Boy, get your ass off of me. You must think I'm that stupid ass sister of mine or the bitch you married. I will get your wig knocked off, nigga. Trust me."

I felt the blows connecting, and all I could do was put my hands up, hoping that they wouldn't reach my face. "Bitch, you should've listened to yo dumb ass sister. I beat bitches." He kept throwing blows on top of blows.

I wanted to scream out, but I couldn't because I was scared it would only infuriate him more. The tears slid down my face as he finally let me go.

"You really put your hands on me?" I looked him dead in the eyes as the tears continued flowing.

"Bitch, you deserved that shit. Oh, yeah, why the fuck you calling Kennedy's phone and shit? Didn't I tell you not to bother that bitch? See, I was trying to be with you, to make you my wife when I get this divorce, but you're hard headed. You're not goin' stop until I fucking leave you alone for good."

"Get out of my house, nigga. I swear it's fucking over."

"Bitch, I ain't going nowhere. Matter-of-fact, go clean yourself up, so I can take yo ass shopping. I've got a few bands to burn on yo ass."

I stood there, looking at him, and realized that he was dead serious. I reluctantly walked off into my room. I glanced at my face in the mirror and realized that my face was swollen, especially by my eyes. I was angry but more hurt.

After I applied some MAC makeup, I was able to hide the bruises and cover up the swelling a little bit. I wasn't in the mood to get dolled up, so I grabbed a pair of my Pink sweatpants from Victoria's Secret and a tank top.

I walked out into the living room where he was seated, looking at his phone. I thought about getting a pot of hot water and throwing it on his ass.

"You ready, babes?"

"Yeah," I barely whispered.

We got into his car, and he pulled off. I thought he was going to take me to Bay Plaza but quickly realized we were going downtown once he got on the Bronx Expressway.

We spent hours shopping in the Village in Manhattan. I got two purses out of the Michael Kors store and a few pairs of jeans and shirts out of the True Religion store. I wasn't goin' lie; the more money he spent, the quicker I was forgiving him.

"I'm tired now," I said to him after we exited Victoria's Secret.

"You sure, ma? Today is your day."

"Yeah, I'm tired and hungry."

"Yeah, I feel you 'cause my belly's touching my back."

After we made it to the car, he placed the bags into the trunk, and we got in and pulled off.

"Aye, yo, I want to apologize about earlier. Man, I don't know what came over me. I think it's because I'm in love with you."

Wait, did I hear this nigga right? Did he say he was in love with me?

"Don't be looking like that. You heard me right. I'm in love with you, B."

I sat quietly, trying to put my words together. I didn't want to say anything that might anger him and bring out his bad side.

"Where were you all these days?"

"Listen, I'ma keep it one hundred one with you. I was over Kennedy's house."

I turned to face him, trying my best not to explode. "Over Kennedy's house? So, you're back with that bitch?"

"Hell nah, I ain't back wit' her ass. I thought we talked about this before. I want what's rightfully mine, half if not everything that the bitch has."

"That was way before I fell for you. I really don't give a fuck about that bitch and her money."

"Yeah, I hear you. You're saying that 'cause you ain't the one that had to fuck that dry pussy bitch e'ery night. Controlled by that bitch. I had to be a fucking puppet for this bitch for years. I deserve all that damn money."

I realized he was serious, and there was nothing I could say that was going to convince him differently.

"So, you're back living with her? I'm confused as fuck right now."

He reached over and grabbed my hand. "Listen, babes, I just need to do this for a little while. I'm going to see a lawyer this week. I'm

Loving Him Ain't Worth A Damn Part 2

filing for a divorce, so I need to make sure that bitch doesn't have anything on me."

"Mmm hmm."

"Please believe me. Picture us living in a big house out in White Plains. With money in the bank, lots of money. You know how you love designer clothes. Baby, I know this bitch; she doesn't like drama, so she's goin' settle for whatever I'm asking for. I need you to ride with me on this, babes. We're in this together." He squeezed my hand.

The wheels were spinning in my head, especially when he said big house up in White Plains. I could definitely see me living amongst the elite. Fuck that hoe. I deserved to be living royally. It didn't take much convincing. I was with him on this.

"So, does that include fucking her?"

"Hell nah. I 'ont want that dry ass pussy that keeps rubbing on my dick like rubber. Matter-of-fact, I've got my own room."

"I just don't want to share that dick."

"Babes, you know that you own this dick. Can't no other bitch out here say I'm fucking them."

I didn't say anything. I really didn't believe him, but I didn't want to let him know that I had doubts.

After we got to the house, he bathed me and fucked me good. I threw the pussy on him extra because I wasn't sure what was going on, but I knew that he would miss this fuck that I gave him. It was getting late, and I was drained, so I decided to get ready for bed. I noticed that he was behaving fidgety.

"Babes, I'm going to lay down. You coming?"

"Nah, I'm about to bounce."

"You serious?" I looked at him.

"Yeah, B. I told you that I've got to pretend like I'm back with this bitch. Yo, don't start tripping, man; just look at the bigger picture. We goin' be rich, babe."

"I hear you." I let out a long sigh and looked at him. I saw that, no matter what I said, it wasn't going to change his mind, so I laid my head on my pillow, feeling helpless.

"Aiight, yo. I'ma hit you later."

"Okay. Just lock the door behind you."

I was feeling irritated as fuck. This nigga beat my ass, and now he was gone back to his little bitch. *What kind of fool does he think I am?* I wondered while a tear fell from my eye.

Loving Him Ain't Worth A Damn Part 2

CHAPTER FIVE

Amoy

The court date for Devon and I was steadily approaching. That must be the reason why his ass kept calling me. I thought about blocking his number but decided to do it after I found out the paternity test results. I swear I'd be happy when this nigga was finally out of my fucking life.

The thought had not left my mind when I heard knocking at the door. I knew it wasn't Marquise because I had just spoken to him, and he was on his way to Queens. I peeked through the peephole and saw two well-dressed females standing there. They looked like they were detectives, but what the fuck would the police want from me? Marquise ran through my mind. I didn't have time to figure the shit out because they started calling my name, I unlocked the deadbolt and opened the door. "Yes, may I help you?"

"Yes, are you Amoy Simpson?"

"Yes, and you are?"

"My name is Miss Warren, and I'm with New York State Child Protective Service."

"Okay, and what do you want with me?"

Out of the corner of my eye, I noticed two officers standing there. I started panicking. What the fuck did CPS and the fucking police want with me? Shit, didn't that have to do with kids and shit?

"May we come in?"

"Uh, I don't… Yeah, sure." I was confused and nervous.

The ladies stepped in, along with the two officers. "Okay, so our office got a report that you have a minor child that was being abused and neglected. In that report, it was also mentioned that there was illegal activities going on from your apartment, including weapons and the dealing of drugs."

"Say what? Who made that report 'cause that shit is a lie?" I blurted out.

"It's our office policy that, whenever we get a report about any kind of abuse against a child, we have to investigate the accusations."

"You know what, lady? I don't know what kind of fucking games y'all playing, but I have one fucking child, and he is sitting right there in his swing, and he ain't getting no type of abuse. As far as drugs and guns, do I look like I'm in these fucking streets?"

"You need to calm down. We are only doing our job," the white officer said.

"Look at my baby." I pointed to my son. "He ain't dirty. He ain't hungry, and he ain't got one damn scratch or mark on him."

Both bitches walked over to my baby and were looking at him and writing some shit on their notepads.

"Ma'am, is it okay if we take a look around?"

I was going to say yes, but then I remembered that the gun that Marquise gave me was under my mattress.

Loving Him Ain't Worth A Damn Part 2

"This is my apartment, and unless you have a warrant, nah, you can't snoop up in here."

"Fair enough but you know this could help your case with CPS."

"I ain't got no damn case... Somebody's lying to y'all asses."

"Well, fair enough, but know this, if we do come back with a warrant, and find anything illegal up in here, I am personally going to drag your ass to jail, and your son will be placed in CPS' custody."

"Get out of my apartment."

"Have a good day, ma'am." The two officers walked out.

"I need to get some information from you."

"Miss Simpson, are you employed?"

"Nah, bitch. I don't work, but does that mean I abuse my fucking child?"

"You need to calm down, talking like this in front of the child."

I rolled my eyes at that hoe and tried to calm my nerves.

"Alright, Miss Simpson. We're done here. You will hear from us after we have concluded our investigation."

I didn't say a damn word. As soon as they exited my shit, I slammed the door shut behind them. To be honest, I acted all hard in front of them, but I was tearing up on the inside. I walked over to my son and took him out of the swing. I held him close to my chest as the tears started to flow like Dunns River Falls in Jamaica. I took a seat on the couch as I trembled.

Racquel Williams

Who the fuck would call these people and do such a horrible thing? Who hated me that fucking much? My stupid ass mama or my conniving ass sister? I needed to know 'cause, when I found out, both them bitches were going to feel these hands.

I grabbed my phone and unblocked Shari's number. "Yo, what the fuck you want, bitch?"

"Did you call CPS on me?"

"Ha ha, nah, you silly bitch. Did they take the little bastard away though?"

"You're a stupid hoe. You know something crazy? How did I ever love and care for you? Treated you like you meant the world to me? You're right, little bitch. I should've left you for dead."

Those were the coldest words that I'd ever had to say to the person that I was supposed to care for the most, but you know what? This time I didn't feel sorry. As a matter-of-fact, I was feeling damn good because I knew there was no way I would ever let her back in my life again.

I went through my phone and blocked her number again. I then hopped onto Facebook and blocked her there too. *RIP LITTLE BITCH!*

Later that night, Marquise came through. I was getting used to this in house dick. It was more than that though. It was the way that he cared for me and my son. It was like he accepted him, even though we weren't sure if he was the father as of yet.

Loving Him Ain't Worth A Damn Part 2

"Yo, babe, is something bothering you?" he asked as I leaned my head on his shoulder as he played his XBOX One.

I raised my head up and let out a long sigh. "Somebody called CPS on me."

"What?" He paused the game and gave me his full attention.

"Yes, the people came here today, talking 'bout how I abused and neglected my child. They also said I have drugs and guns around him."

"Man, why you ain't call me?"

"I know you in them streets. I didn't want to disturb you."

"Man, fuck these streets. You're my woman, and anything that has to do wit' you is more important than anything. Did they say who did that shit?"

"Nah. The police even asked me if he could search the apartment. I told his ass hell nah."

"You did right, baby. Unless they've got a warrant, they can't just come up in here. By the way, where is that hammer that I gave you?"

"In my room, under the bed."

"Aiight, cool. I'ma take it up outta here. You never know what they've got up their sleeves. I 'ont want you to get involved in no bullshit."

"Yeah, I feel you."

"So, what they goin' do?"

"I don't know. I know it's a lie. I think my mama or my sister got something to do wit' it though."

"You think so? I was thinking it was that fuck nigga. You know these niggas nowadays be acting just like bitches."

Until he said that, I really didn't think it was Devon, but seeing how he was behaving lately, I wouldn't put it past him.

We talked for a little while and then smoked a few blunts together. I was feeling blessed that he was back in my life. I couldn't help but wonder how long this fairy tale was going to last because I felt like I was cursed from the day I exited that crack head bitch's bad luck pussy.

***

"Bae, you ready?" Marquise yelled.

It was my court day. He told me the night before that he was definitely going with me 'cause he knew Devon was going to be present. I looked at myself in the mirror and walked out to the living room where Jamal and him were waiting.

"Bout damn time, B."

"Boy, hush. You know I had to make sure my hair was on point."

"Yeah, whatever. Let's go."

We walked out of the door, and I locked the door behind us. I was kind of nervous, but after the beating that nigga put on me, there was no way I was going to miss his court date.

"Yo, you goin' be straight. I love you, girl," he said as he reached over and grabbed my sweaty hand.

"Love you too." This was the first time that I said it back to him.

Loving Him Ain't Worth A Damn Part 2

We got to the courthouse a few minutes before nine. He parked, and we walked in. I looked around me, but I didn't see Devon, which was great because I didn't want a confrontation between him and Marquise. We entered the courtroom, and there they were. That nigga and my dumb ass sister sitting beside him. My blood started boiling, just seeing them together. Marquise must've felt it too because he placed his arm around me. "Come sit over here, bae."

I saw when my sister whispered something in Devon's ear, and he turned around and stared at us. Marquise smirked at him. He smiled in return, but it wasn't one of those friendly smiles. It was more like a devilish grin.

The bailiff entered the courtroom, and that broke up the drama that was brewing.

"All rise. The Honorable Judge Hudson presiding."

My body was present, but my mind wasn't as I remembered the day that nigga beat the hell out of me. I was here for his trial and to make sure I told my side of the story.

To my surprise, the coward decided to plead guilty. I couldn't believe I heard right. Instead of facing me on the stand, this bitch ass nigga entered a guilty plea in exchange for a little bit of time. Who the fuck decided this shit? Why wasn't I notified of this ahead of time? God knew I wouldn't have wasted my time by coming here today. The judge set a date for his sentencing, and just like that, it was over. I waited to speak to the D.A.

Racquel Williams

"Hello, Miss Simpson."

"Why did you accept that plea?" I confronted the D.A. that was handling the case.

"This was a hard case to prove. It was your word against his, and with your sister willing to testify that you told her it was someone else, if we had gone to trial, there was a possibility that he could've walked. With the plea bargain, I will be asking for prison time, up to eighteen months."

"Eighteen months? Lady, did you look at the pictures? Did you see how bad he beat me? But y'all don't care 'cause it didn't happen to y'all. What does it take? That nigga killing me for y'all to take me serious? Because he's dangerous as hell and he is allowed to walk these streets," I lashed out.

"I understand you fully, Miss Simpson. Even with the plea, he will get some prison time, and now you can secure a permanent restraining order against him."

I looked at that bitch and shook my head. Whose side was she on anyway? I had a feeling that all of these motherfuckers were buddy buddy.

"Let's go," I turned and said to Marquise.

He picked up my son, and we left that bitch standing there, looking like a damn fool.

We were about to go up the stairs when I heard Devon's voice.

"Now you got this nigga carrying my son and shit?"

Loving Him Ain't Worth A Damn Part 2

I turned around to face this nigga. "Your son? The one that you don't even know. Have you even bought a pamper or, fuck that, a McDonald's kids' meal? Yes, this nigga can carry him 'cause guess why? He tucks him in at night. He buys him pampers, sneakers, and clothes. He makes sure he eats."

"You're a stupid ass hoe."

Marquise put little man down and took a few steps down. I jumped in front of him. "Nah, what you doing? You see where we at? This nigga ain't worth it. Trust me, he's pussy, just like the bitch he's standing beside."

"Ha ha, you're funny. Bitch, you know I'll beat that ass. I done told bae not to trust your nasty, pussy selling ass."

I stood there, laughing in that bitch's face. Another place or time, I would've torn her little, young ass up.

"Yo, son, this the second time this hoe saved you. The next time, you won't be that lucky," Devon said, winking at Marquise and then walking off.

The walk to the car was quiet. I was furious that this bitch kept on trying me. I swear, I just wanted one chance, just one, to show her she wasn't built like that.

After I strapped Jamal in his seat, I got in, and he pulled off. "Yo, B. I know that nigga might be Jamal's father and shit, but I'ma have to dead that nigga. He done threatened my life more than once. I 'ont take no threat lightly, and I'll bust a cap in a nigga before he gets at me first."

"I'm sorry that I brought you into my drama."

"Man, cut that shit out. You ain't did nothing but give the pussy to a lame ass nigga."

"Yeah, if only I knew how he was goin' turn out."

"And I know that's yo sister and shit, but that lil bitch needs her ass beat."

"Man, I swear I'm still shocked that she's carrying it like that. I don't really care though. Fuck her."

I meant every word of that.

"Listen, boo, we need to get that test done. I'm going to set an appointment."

"What test?"

"The paternity test."

"Oh, aiight. Yeah, go ahead and do that."

"God, please don't let my baby be Devon's son," I whispered under my breath.

Loving Him Ain't Worth A Damn Part 2

KENNEDY

This nigga had the nerve to ask me if I could go to court with him. Nah, his exact words were, "It would be a good look if my wife went to court with me." So, you mean to tell me that this nigga beat his side bitch up, and he wanted me, Kennedy, to make a fool out of myself by going to court with him? Ha ha, I almost choked, laughing at that ridiculous idea.

I noticed him sitting at my kitchen table when I walked in from getting groceries. I tried my best to ignore him as I spotted him staring at me.

"So, you ain't goin' ask me what happened in court today?"

"Why should I? That's your business," I said as I washed the grapes in vinegar and water.

"Damn, Kennedy, why are you so cold towards me? I mean, a nigga knows he fucked up, but I'm home now, and I told you that I regret ever fooling around on you."

"So, you think that you disrespected your vows and made a fucking, illegitimate bastard and, because you say you're sorry, we should forget all about that and move on?"

"What else can I do? Name it. I'll do whatever you want me to do, and I done told you that bitch's lying. That ain't my damn baby. She's broke and trying to get money up out of me."

"Money? Hmmm…"

I was about to say, "Nigga, you're broke as hell," but I decided to keep my mouth shut.

He got off of his stool and walked over to me. "Listen, Kennedy, baby. You're my wife, my soulmate, my best friend. I'm a man, and I fucked up, but please don't hold this against me. This is what that bitch wants. She wants you to leave me, thinking I'll be back over there. Yo, B. I love you, and if I can't have you then I don't want to be fucking alive."

He grabbed my hand and fell to his knees. "Please, baby, forgive me. I can be the man that you want me to be if you just show me."

"You look fucking weak right now, and you know how much I despise weak ass men."

"I don't care how the fuck I look right now. I fucking love you, and I don't care if I look like a bitch."

He stood up and started rubbing on me. God knew I was trying to back up, but this nigga and his hands always managed to keep me hostage.

They say that break up and make up sex was the best. It had been months since I gave him the pussy, and no lie, my love hole was missing his ass, or more like his dick, like a motherfucker. His chocolate body was very enticing in that wife beater. He palmed the bottom of my ass as he stuck his tongue down my throat. My brain was telling me to push his trifling ass off of me, but my pussy and my heart were in cahoots.

Loving Him Ain't Worth A Damn Part 2

"Ugh, don't touch me, Devon," I snapped with an attitude.

I guess he said, "Fuck that shit she's talking," because he wrapped his arms around my waist and pressed his hard dick against my body.

"Kennedy, babe, don't act like that," he whispered into my ear, followed by a kiss.

"Stop, Devonnn, you know that's my spot," I whined like a baby.

He continued to kiss around my ear, and then he slid his fingers down my shorts, into my wetness.

"Sssss, stop it," I moaned.

There was no way I was going to stop him. My pussy was so moist and wet, and his dick was yearning for my sweet, chocolate pussy. He licked his finger, tasting my juices while he stared in my eyes. I unzipped his pants and slid his dick out of his boxers. I was truly missing Devon's sex, no matter how many side bitches he had. I was battling with different emotions. I sure hated his ass for the shit he did to me, and then I was loving the way he was finessing my body.

"Stop it, Devon. You know I hate your ass right about now."

He totally ignored my pleas. He slid my panties to the side and squeezed his dick into my wetness, lifting me up and wrapping my legs around his waist. "Oh, shit, babe. I miss you so much," he whispered in my ear as he sunk his manhood deeper inside of me, penetrating into my goodies.

"Sssss, I hate you so damn much," I moaned. He carried me while he was still inside of me. He put me down and slid out; he then turned me around on the couch.

My back was arched perfectly as he gripped my shoulders to keep me from running from the dick.

"I hate you. I fuckin' hate you," I moaned louder and louder, at the same time backing it up on his dick.

He didn't ease up any as he applied pressure. I finally decided to stop fighting the feeling and loosen up. He started slapping my ass. "You hate me, huh?" He slapped my ass harder and jammed every inch of his dick into my pussy. His balls smacked against my ass with each thrust he took.

"I love you, Devon. I fucking love you." I sang a new tune while I felt his dick go in and out of my wetness. He continued slapping my ass, and I screamed out in ecstasy.

"Oh, shit Kennedy. Ooooo, shit," he groaned.

My pussy muscles gripped his dick. I threw the pussy back like a champ, and I was definitely the most valuable player. His veins got bigger; he grabbed me aggressively, and seconds later, his dick was spitting out cum like a sprinkler.

After he pulled out, I hurriedly ran up the stairs. I couldn't believe that I allowed this to happen. But wait, I actually liked it, so why was I feeling like this? "Kennedy, get out your feelings," my inner voice scolded.

Loving Him Ain't Worth A Damn Part 2

I got off of the bed and decided to take a shower. I was slipping, though, because I should've made him use a condom. I was too old to be having a burning pussy.

***

After I took my shower, I decided to finish unpacking my groceries. Shit, the ice cream that I bought was left on the counter and was melted. I threw it in the trash and wiped the counter off. I thought about throwing something in the oven, but to be honest, after getting fucked that good, all my energy was gone. I had to remind myself that I was no longer in my twenties.

I didn't see Devon after we had sex. I assumed that he was in his room, trying to recoup from beating up this pussy.

After warming up some Progresso Clam Chowder soup, I decided to lay down and relax. I grabbed the remote, trying to catch an episode of *Criminal Minds* on A&E. Before I could rest my head on the pillow, my phone started ringing.

"Hello."

"Hey there, beautiful." Christopher's voice caught me off guard.

"Hey you. How you doing?"

"I got that info you requested the other day."

I took a second, trying to remember what info he was supposed to get for me. It quickly flashed in my head.

"Oh, shit. I totally forgot about that."

"Yeah, I was tied up on another case; that's why I didn't get with you sooner."

"So, are you going to email it to me?"

"I was thinking about dropping by, so I can make sweet love to your mind and soul. You know I can make that thing wet," he chuckled.

All of a sudden, I didn't feel too good. "No, Chris, I need to take a rain check. I'm a little bit under the weather."

"I can come over and make you some homemade soup," he persisted.

"Christopher, no. I'm just going to sleep."

"Alright. I'll email you the information."

"Thank you, Chris."

I hung up the phone, sort of feeling bad that I was so short with him. But there was no way I could invite him over, knowing Devon was here. I thought I'd made a big mistake when I allowed him to fuck me the other day.

I am too tired to stress over all this shit right now. Tomorrow I'll figure out a way to make it up to Christopher, I thought before I dozed off.

Loving Him Ain't Worth A Damn Part 2

SHARI

The last couple of days, I'd noticed that when I peed, it started burning. At first, I thought it was only because Devon and I had sex, and he tore my ass up as usual. But this morning, we didn't have sex, and when I went to pee, the pain had become unbearable, to the point where I couldn't move. On top of that, a foul smell was coming out of my pussy when I stuck my finger in there.

I got dressed and decided to go to the clinic on Fourth Street. As I sat there, waiting to be called, I couldn't help but wonder what the hell was going on. I was a bitch that loved getting head, so I tried my best to keep my shit on point at all times. Devon... Fuck, I totally forgot about old boy that I fucked the other day. Shit, I didn't make that nigga wear a condom. *Oh, fuck*, I thought...

"Miss Simpson," the nurse finally called my name after about forty-five minutes of waiting.

I followed her into the room. "What brings you in today?"

"I need to do some tests. I think I've got something."

"Please be more specific."

"I think I've got some sort of STD."

"What symptoms are you experiencing?"

"Burning and painful urination and, oh yeah, a fishy smell."

"Are you sexually active, and how many partners do you have?"

"Listen, lady, I've only got one. Okay?" I was getting irritated with all these damn questions. As a matter-of-fact, my ass really didn't want to be here.

"Put this gown on and remove everything from the waist down. The doctor will be in shortly. Here goes a cup. Pee in it and put it in the window."

Soon after she left the room, I quickly took my clothes off. I was ready for this process to be over with quickly. Ten minutes later, the doctor walked in, and I told his ass the same shit I told the nurse. He placed me on the bed and examined me. He also took samples to send to the lab.

"Miss Simpson, it seems like you have gonorrhea. I am sending off the samples to the lab, and those tests won't be back for a few days. I'm going to give you a single dose of 250mg of intramuscular Ceftriaxone and 1g of oral Azithromycin. Please advise your partner so he can also get texted and treated. Until this is cleared up, please refrain from having sexual intercourse. Also, your pregnancy test came back positive."

"What?" I looked at him.

"Congrats on your pregnancy. It's best for you to follow up with your doctor to start getting prenatal care."

I wasn't really paying attention to what the fuck he was saying. I was going straight to the abortion clinic ASAP.

Loving Him Ain't Worth A Damn Part 2

After I left out of their office, I hurried to my car. I was tight as fuck because I knew one of these niggas gave this shit to me. Which one of them was the million-dollar question. I wanted to call both of them, but if I called the wrong one, it would be proven that I was fucking around. My head started hurting. I hoped I didn't give this shit to Devon, or it could possibly be his ass that gave that shit to me. I needed a way to find out who gave this shit to me.

As far as being pregnant, I could tell Devon that I was pregnant, and we could have our own little family since Amoy's baby wasn't really his in the first place. I smiled as I thought about how freaking brilliant that idea was.

I stopped by the grocery store to pick up some chicken breasts. I looked up a recipe on YouTube, and I was going to try it. Shit, it wouldn't be a five star meal, but hey, with this good news that I was about to give him, shit, he couldn't help but be grateful that a bitch was trying.

I got my items, paid, and walked out. I dialed Devon's number to let him know I was cooking, but his phone went straight to voicemail. Here this nigga was with this bullshit. I threw the phone on the passenger seat and cut the music on. I was trying my best not to get irritated because I knew what he was trying to get done. I just wished he would just kill the bitch and get it over with already.

CHAPTER SIX

Amoy

"**D**ear God, I know I haven't been the best, but I come to you as humbly as I possibly can. God, I need to ask you this one favor; please let Marquise be the father of my son. I know I should've been more careful, but if you're going to punish someone, please punish me for my sins and not my baby. My baby needs a father that can provide and teach him to be a man. God, please, I'm begging you." I got off of my knees and wiped the tears away from my eyes. I swear I needed this one miracle.

"Listen, bae, I know you're nervous and shit, but we need to know this." He squeezed my hand as we walked to the building. A week ago, I scheduled for us to go in and get the test done.

We had to wait a few weeks to get the results back, and those were the worst couple weeks of my life. I kept wondering how I was going to deal with this nigga, Devon, if he turned out to be my son's father and, most importantly, how the relationship between Marquise and my son was going to be if Jamal wasn't his child.

I knew he said he would still be here, but at this moment, that was all talk. I guess that was the bed that I made…

***

I finally got a call back from a salon in the Bronx. I would be braiding hair and doing the shampooing. It wasn't much right now, but it would help me to make a few coins while I got into beauty school. I

Loving Him Ain't Worth A Damn Part 2

knew Marquise was spending his money, but shit, I wasn't sure how long it would last. I was excited as hell to share this news with him.

I pulled up and parked in my parking space. Before I could run into the apartment, I noticed the mailman pulling up, so I turned back around. I had no idea why because all I ever received was damn bills, and it was sure bill time again. "Miss Pam, you got anything for me?" I asked as I approached the mail lady.

"Hmm, let's see." She dug through her mail. "Yup. Here you go." She handed me three pieces of mail.

"Thank you."

I took them and walked off. I noticed the big envelope, so I decided to open it up first. I stopped dead in my tracks. *You're excluded as the biological father of Devon Jamal Guthrie JR. The probability of paternity is 0%.*

I read it over and over, and it was still saying the same thing. My head started feeling dizzy. How could this be? God, no! I leaned on my front door as I tried to digest this bullshit. A few minutes later, I wiped my tears and opened the door.

"Hey, bae." Marquise greeted me as soon as I walked in the door.

I noticed he was sitting there, playing the game with little man sitting on his lap, pretending like he was playing also. I couldn't find the words to say anything. Instead, I flopped down beside him on the couch. "You aiight, bae?"

I shoved the paper at him.

"What's this?" he quizzed.

Before I could respond, he had already started reading. He took little man off of his leg and paused the game. He stood up, took another look at the paper, and walked off. I got up and followed him into the hallway.

"Man, how the fuck could this be? They wrong, bae. They fucking wrong. That nigga ain't no damn father. I am, B," he yelled as he hit the wall.

I didn't know what to say to him. I was hurting just as much as him or even more. I wrapped my arms around him as I felt a tear drop on my arm.

"Babe, listen, I'm so sorry. I didn't mean for this to happen," I said while tears started to flow.

"That nigga don't know shit about him. He's too busy to even check on him. How the fuck he a father, huh?"

"I know, baby... I'm just as shocked as you." I hugged him tighter.

He turned around to face me. He pulled me closer and hugged me. "Listen, B. I don't give a fuck what them white people shit say. This my motherfucking son, and I ain't goin' nowhere."

We hugged each other, crying, until we both heard little man.

"Mama."

Marquise let me go and picked Jamal up. "Yo, you're my son, and that's law," he said to my son and hugged him tight.

Loving Him Ain't Worth A Damn Part 2

It broke my heart to see this man in so much pain. As a matter-of-fact, this was my first time seeing him this emotional. He was always this hard, street nigga, but right now, I was definitely seeing another side of him. A side that was calmer and genuine.

Now that I knew he wasn't the father, I knew the only other option was Devon. It hurt my stomach just to think that his blood was running through my son's veins. I thought about not telling him, but I wasn't that type of person, and I wouldn't dare keep him away from his child. I was hoping the bum would give up his rights, but knowing him, it was all about control, and he would not give me the satisfaction.

After we calmed down from the shock, we decided to order something to eat. Jamal ate, and I gave him a bath. We watched cartoons with him, but before the cartoon was over, he was knocked out. I took him to his room and tucked him in. I returned to the living room to chill with Marquise. I knew we were both feeling fucked up behind the results, but there wasn't anything that I could really do about it.

We ended up getting fucked up after smoking blunt after blunt and drinking Grey Goose. That night, we didn't have sex; instead, he just held me as we both got lost in our thoughts.

***

After I dropped Jamal at daycare, and Marquise left for the day, I decided to give Devon a call.

"Yo, what the fuck you callin' my line fo?" His arrogant ass answered the phone.

"Boy, whatever. I did the paternity test on Jamal. Marquise ain't the father, so that leaves you as the only other option."

"Bitch, you're silly as fuck. So, you mean to tell me, this whole time you had me believing I was the father, and now, you're telling me you had to do a test. You're a bigger hoe than I thought."

"You know what? I was so praying that you weren't his father because you're a no good ass nigga. All I want from you is for you to sign over your fucking rights, so I don't ever have to deal with you again," I lashed out.

"Bitch, I ain't signing shit. Fuck you. Matter-of-fact, I will be taking your ass to court for full custody. There's no way I'ma let you raise my son around that bitch ass nigga. And, oh yeah, hoe, you need to find somewhere else to lay your head. I want you out of my shit."

"Your shit?"

"Yeah, bitch. Did you forget that I was the one that got it for you in the first place? Ungrateful ass hoe."

I hung up on his ass while steaming with anger. This nigga deserved to die for real. I sat on the bed, trying to calm myself down. I swear I had no idea how the fuck I allowed myself to even fuck this bitch ass nigga.

I dialed Marquise's number. "Hey, babes. You aiight?"

"No, I'm not. I swear I hate Devon's ass." I cried into the phone.

Loving Him Ain't Worth A Damn Part 2

"Why? What that fuck nigga did? Did he do something to hurt you?" He bombarded me with questions.

"I called his ass to tell him that I thought he was the father, and that nigga went off, calling me all kinds of names. Then, he's talking about he goin' take me to court for full custody. I swear, boo, if he comes near my child, I'ma kill his ass."

"Babe, listen to me. That pussy nigga ain't goin' do shit. He's just trying to scare you. Man, if that nigga ever does anything to hurt you, I'ma bury his ass."

"I just need to move for real and get away from him."

"Yeah, I feel you, bae. But aye, I'm out here in these streets. I'ma hit you back later."

"Okay, love you."

"Love you, bae."

I hung the phone up and laid back on the bed. I needed to move out of this place ASAP. I didn't have all of the money, so later, I planned on asking Marquise for help.

Racquel Williams

KENNEDY

I checked my email and saw what Christopher sent to me. It was a picture and an address. I sat there, staring at the bitch that called my number, looking for my husband. It was crazy because she resembled the bitch that I visited before. Matter-of-fact, they could pass for twins. What kind of crazy joke was this? Was this the same bitch?

I grabbed my phone and called Christopher. "Hello there, pretty lady."

"Christopher, this picture that you sent me... are you sure this is the person?"

"Yes, I'm one hundred percent sure. I followed her around for a few days, and I also caught a few pics of your husband going in and out of her apartment. Is something wrong?"

"Nah, maybe I'm just tripping... But there's a slight resemblance between the bitch that has the baby and this one."

"I thought the same thing at first, and after digging around, I found out they're sisters."

"You're fucking lying, Christopher," I yelled out.

"No, ma'am. I'm pretty sure they are. The one with the baby is the oldest."

"What a dog. You mean to tell me, my husband is fucking two sisters and has a baby by one? Wow, fucking amazing."

"I told you his ass has been busy."

Loving Him Ain't Worth A Damn Part 2

"I see. Anyway, I will call you later. I just had to make sure I wasn't tripping."

"Alrighty. Talk to you later."

After we hung up, I put the address in my phone. I grabbed my purse and headed out the door. I knew that, maybe, I should leave this alone, but I refused to. I needed to know every little bit of dirt this nigga was doing. I walked downstairs, where he was in the living room, playing music.

"I'm heading out for a little while," I yelled over the music.

"Where you off to? Do you need me to go with you?"

"No, I'm just running down to the bank. I'll be back in a few. Maybe we can grab something to eat at Fridays later."

"Aiight, babes. Sounds like a plan. Be careful out there, and remember I love you." He came over and kissed me.

I smiled at him as I hurried out the door. I got in the car and pulled off. I was on a mission.

I pulled up to the apartment complex, parked, and walked to the building. I realized that I had to walk up the damn stairs. *Fuck*, I thought as I started climbing these damn stairs.

I reached the apartment and knocked. I had no idea what I was going to say to get in here.

"Who is it?" she yelled.

"It's Kennedy." I decided not to beat around the bush.

There were a few seconds of silence, and then I heard the locks unlocking, and the door flew wide open.

"Look at what we've got here." She stood there, one hand on her waist and the other holding the door.

"So, I see you remember who I am, and since we're both grown, how about I step inside?"

She moved out of the way and used her hand to motion me to step inside.

"So, what can I do for you? Isn't your husband back home with you?"

"Yes, that two timing ass bastard is back at the house. As far as with me, I doubt that."

"Well, what the fuck you want with me?"

"What I want from you is for you to tell me how long you've been screwing my husband?"

"Don't you think you should be asking your husband these questions?"

"Listen to me, little bitch. We both know the nigga is a dog. Matter-of-fact, isn't he fucking your sister also? Oops, did you know about that?"

"Listen, Kennedy, or whatever your fucking name is, I don't give a fuck if that nigga's fucking you, my sister, or a got damn dog. All I care about is when he's fucking me."

Loving Him Ain't Worth A Damn Part 2

"Nonsense! You're putting up this hard façade, but I see through it. Matter-of-fact, I've been through this kind of shit before. You know when you love a man and, in your heart, you're hoping that he'll leave all those other women that he's sleeping with. I've been there, so I feel your pain, but baby girl, it's all empty promises."

"Bitch, you think you know me, huh? I'm nothing like you or my motherfucking sister. Matter-of-fact, you're the one that married him, not me. So while you're over here, preaching to me like you're a fucking saint, shouldn't you be worried about who your husband is fucking right now? Cause guess what? I ain't worried."

"Ha ha, little girl. One thing I've learned in my years of dealing with men is that, if he's going to cheat, he's going to do it, and there's nothing me or the next woman can do to stop him. See, the difference between you and I is that I don't need that cheating ass bastard, so like a sick puppy, he will always run back to me."

"Yeah, right... I might not be old and wrinkled like yo ass, but trust me, I do know that you're worried about that nigga 'cause, if yo ass wasn't, you would be laying up comfortably in yo big ass house and not standing in my living room, trying to convince me that you don't want him."

"You know what's wrong with us women? Instead of us sticking together, and stopping these cheating ass niggas, we lie for them, give them pussy, and let them dog us out. You're still young, and you've got a long way to go…. It might not be today, but karma's going to bite you in the ass. That nigga ain't shit, and you will find out in due time."

"Listen, I don't want to hear shit you've got to say. From my understanding, the nigga's back over there with you. So, go on home, put that old wrinkled ass pussy on him, and make him happy… I don't have shit else to say to you, so please lose my fucking address. Oh, by the way, how do you know where I live?"

"How would I get it? You're the smart dummy. I'll let myself out."

I took one last look at the bitch and walked to the door. I unlocked it and let myself out. I was disgusted with Devon and how he disrespected me.

Loving Him Ain't Worth A Damn Part 2

SHARI

I was past irritated that this bitch showed up where the fuck I lived at. Number one, how the fuck did she know where I laid my head at, and why would she think it was cool to pop up at my shit, just because we were fucking the same nigga? As soon as I saw her pull off, I grabbed my phone.

The phone rang a few times and then went straight to voicemail. I didn't ease up any. I kept redialing the number.

"Yo, man, what the fuck you blowing me up for, like you're dying or something."

"Shit, nigga, I know you see me calling you," I said, sounding irritated.

"Mane, you know I'm at the crib, and I can't be on the phone like that in the daytime. I don't want ole girl to think that I'm on no bullshit."

"Hmm, that's strange."

"What's strange?"

"You claiming that you're at home, and you're worried about that bitch hearing you on the phone, but her ass just left from over here."

"Say what? Who just left from over there?"

"Mmm hmm. Nigga, you're too funny. You know what? Go ahead and play them damn games by yourself."

I didn't wait for a response. I just hung the phone up. That nigga sat there, telling a whole lie, not knowing that bitch was just over here.

Racquel Williams

I swear I didn't know what to make of this dude. One second, it seemed like he loved me, and we were going to work it out, but as soon as I started believing in him, he'd do something that made me question how solid he really was.

"Hello. Man, what you want?" I answered the third time he called back.

"I'm on the way over, B." This time, he hung up before I could respond.

I just shook my head and threw the phone down. *Oh, now he wants to fly over here 'cause his bitch was here. Tell you about his flip flop ass*, I thought as I cut the TV on. I was gone all day and didn't get a chance to watch *Paternity Court*. Shit, I might be having my own case of paternity court going on.

"Open the door, man." I heard him yelling and banging.

I opened the door and looked at him like he'd lost his fucking mind.

"Yo, you do know I've got neighbors. Why are you out here behaving like this?"

"Man, you shoulda opened this shit when I first knocked."

I was going to argue, but I remembered what took place the last time that we got into it. I swear I wasn't trying to get my ass beat again.

I took a seat on the couch, pretending like I was still watching television.

100

Loving Him Ain't Worth A Damn Part 2

"Yo, why'd you hang the phone up when I was trying to talk to you?"

"Because, boy, all you do is lie, lie, lie. I mean, I'm tired of all the bullshit you're dishing out. I mean, I know what the fuck you say you're doing, but your actions are screaming differently."

"Man, c'mon, B. Do I have to keep going over the same damn thing? So, what did Kennedy say to you?"

"Nah, the question is why did you give this bitch my address?"

"Man, what? I ain't give nobody yo damn address and definitely not her."

"I don't know what kind of games y'all playing, but y'all need to keep that shit over there at y'all house."

"Yo, B, I'm dead ass serious. I didn't give her your address or discuss you with her. So, what the fuck she say?" He seemed agitated.

"Why don't you ask her? I mean, you her husband and shit. Remember, I'm just the side bitch."

"Yo, B, cut it, man. You know what? I don't need this shit. Maybe y'all two can get together and suck on each other's pussy. I'm out."

"You're so fucking disrespectful. I swear."

"Disrespectful? You keep playing kiddie games and shit. Like you want me to beg you. Nah, B. I'm a grown ass man, and I ain't got time for y'all childish games. I'm out."

I really thought he was bluffing or trying my hand to see if I would fold. Shit got real when he opened the door and walked out. I jumped off the couch and ran out the door after him. "Devon, wait. You can't go." I grabbed the back of his shirt.

"Man, get off me," he said and tried to get away from me.

"Please don't go. I'm pregnant."

He stopped suddenly and turned around to face me. "You what?"

"I'm pregnant, bae."

"Man, it ain't mine."

I let go of his shirt. "What the fuck you mean it ain't yours? You're the only nigga I been fucking."

"Man, you know what? I'm sorry, babe. You just caught me off guard."

He stepped closer and hugged me. *Yeah, that's more like it*, I thought.

"Come inside. Let me talk to you." He grabbed my hand and led me inside.

I knew he would see things my way once I told him I was pregnant. He took a seat on the couch. "Come here. Sit right here."

I took a seat on his lap. He took my hands into his hands.

"You pregnant for real?"

"Yes, I went to the doctor today."

"Damn, babe. How far along are you?"

"I'm not sure. I need to do a follow up with my primary care doctor."

"For what? You having an abortion, right?"

Loving Him Ain't Worth A Damn Part 2

I jumped off that nigga's leg and stood over him. "What the fuck you just ask me?"

"I mean, c'mon, you know what I'm trying to do. I can't be having no more babies popping out."

"No more babies? So now you're claiming my sister's little bastard?"

"You ain't heard?"

"Heard what?"

"The paternity test came back that the other nigga ain't the daddy."

"And what? You think you're automatically the daddy? I can't believe you're so naïve. That bitch was a pussy selling whore. Anybody can be the damn daddy, but here you are, thinking you're special 'cause she said you're the daddy."

"Damn, B. You sound bitter as fuck. How do you want to be my woman, but you're not willing to accept my seed?"

"Boy, I hate that bitch, and I hate anything that is part of her, including that fucking baby. You can go ahead and play daddy. That ain't got nothing to do with our relationship. I'm fucking you, not your child."

"Yo, this been on my mind for a long time, so I'm curious... Were you always this hateful towards your sister, or you just developed this?"

"Hate? Nah, let me correct you. I despise this bitch. You know, when I was younger, I looked up to that bitch; matter-of-fact, I wanted to be like that bitch. But the older I got, I realized how selfish that bitch was. She only cared for self, so I started developing my hate for her."

"Damn B. that's deep. I wish I had known that y'all were sisters…"

"What? You wouldn't have fucked with me, nigga?" I cut him off before he got to talking stupid.

"I'm just saying… y'all need to mend y'all relationship."

"So now you give a fuck? Ha ha, you're a funny nigga. If you care so fucking much, you would've left, but you didn't. So guess what? Yo ass ain't no good either. I don't give a fuck about all this that you're talking 'bout. I got my own shit to worry about."

"Aiight, man. Chill out wit' all this. We need to figure out what we're goin' to do."

"Nah, I know what I'm doing. The question is what you goin' to do?"

"You're not thinking rationally right now. You're going off emotions."

"Really, Devon? Why you don't just kill the bitch? It's much easier than you playing house and shit. Yo ass might still lose. That bitch ain't no fool."

Loving Him Ain't Worth A Damn Part 2

"Yeah, I've been thinking 'bout that too. I just know I'm the first person they're gonna look at if something was to happen to her, and considering my track record..."

"Man, if we go ahead and plan this shit out, trust me, they can't tie you to anything. Plus, I'll be yo alibi. See, they know you were fucking my sister, not me."

"Well... let's think this out clearly. It would be good to get this out of my life permanently and still get all of her fucking money. That bitch is damn near a millionaire."

"Yes, now you're talking, babe. We're goin' to be some rich motherfuckers. We can push that bitch down the stairs, and make it seem like her old ass fell, or we can find somebody to shoot that bitch in the head." I giggled.

"Like I said, I can't do it because I'm going to be the first suspect on their list. But I know a few niggas that are hungry and will definitely take that bitch out for the right price. I'ma do some thinking. Listen, don't ever text me or talk about this on the phone. You know that's how niggas be getting caught up in some bullshit."

"Trust me, I know. I watch a lot of shows on the ID Channel."

"Aiight, cool. I've got to get back to the house and play husband. I love you, yo. In the meantime, you need to think about getting an abortion. C'mon, babe, we've still got our whole lives ahead of us, and if a baby is involved, they might say that's why I killed her. Trust me, I know how these motherfuckers operate."

He stood up and grabbed me towards him. "Listen, yo, you're my woman, so quit getting in your feelings and shit. I ain't goin' nowhere, just like yo ass ain't goin' nowhere. You hear me?"

"Yeah, I hear you," I said nonchalantly.

He started kissing me passionately. I placed my hands around his neck and kissed him back. I wasn't listening to none of that nonsense he was spitting. I was more worried about the money that we were going to get after this bitch died.

Loving Him Ain't Worth A Damn Part 2

CHAPTER SEVEN

Kennedy

"Doctor, I know what you just said, but I'm telling you you're wrong. There's no way I've got no damn gonorrhea. Do you see my age? I ain't had that shit in my twenties, so I know damn well there's no way I've got it now."

"Mrs. Guthrie, I examined you, and I listened to you tell me the symptoms that you're feeling, and this is what it sounds like. You said you're sexually active, so it could possibly be from your partner."

"Doctor, listen, how long does it take for those other tests to come back?"

"Three or four days at the most. If there's anything, you will receive a call from us for you to come in. In the meantime, I'm going to give you a single shot of an antibiotic called Ceftriaxone, along with a second oral antibiotic called Doxycycline. Please don't have sex while you're being treated, and you might want to tell your partner, so he can get tested also. If he doesn't get treatment, he'll just re-infect you."

I didn't say much. Instead, I just laid my head back on the examining table. I was too lost for words to even say anything, and to be honest, what was I going to say? I was a fucking fool.

After I left the doctor's office, I headed straight home. I was too fucking pissed to say the least. I fucked two men; one used a condom and one didn't, so there was no reason for me to guess which one of them had a burning dick. I shook my head; I was disgusted as hell. Never had I ever had to go in no doctor's office, telling them my pussy was on fire until now. I was doing one hundred miles per hour, trying to get home.

***

I pulled into the driveway and quickly turned the car off. I grabbed my purse and rushed up the stairs. I was so mad that I forgot to check if his car was parked in the front. I rushed up the stairs. First, I looked in my room. He wasn't there, so I rushed to his room. I tried to bust in, but the door was locked.

I started banging on the door with my fist. I wanted to break this shit off the hinges. "Open this fucking door, Devon," I yelled out.

"Damn, bae, I didn't hear you come in. What's going on?"

"What's going on? Your dirty dick ass done gave me a fucking STD."

"What the hell you talking 'bout, Kennedy? I ain't gave you shit."

I took the paper out of my purse and threw it at him. "See there. I've got gonorrhea, and you're the only man that I'm sleeping with."

"You sure about that? Remember I was gone for a while, and you had that other nigga all up in here. Maybe his ass gave that shit to you 'cause I ain't got shit. My dick is perfectly fine," he chuckled.

"You know, I really thought we had a chance, but you're not even man enough to admit when you're wrong. I know you gave me this

108

shit because you're nasty, and you were running up in them hoes without a condom."

"Kennedy, baby, I swear I'm a changed man. I told you, if you gave me another chance, I would not cheat anymore, and I mean that. I'll go get tested tomorrow, but I doubt that I have anything."

I looked at him, shook my head, and walked away. I wanted to throw his ass out, but that wouldn't make sense. I had a plan…

***

I was lying down in my room, just thinking about life. I needed a change of scenery. Lately, I'd been thinking about relocating to Florida. My oldest sister, Flora, lived in Fort Lauderdale, and for years, she had been asking me to move down there. I was a New York girl and never thought of leaving. But what was really here for me? Nothing, not after all the shit that I'd been through for the last few months. I was ready to sell these houses and buy me a house in Florida. Truth was, I wasn't getting any younger and needed to start thinking about my golden years.

The ringing of my cell phone interrupted my thoughts. I reached over and grabbed it up. I really wasn't in the mood to talk to anyone right now.

"Hello."

"Hey there, beautiful."

"Hey there."

"I'm calling you to invite you to my house for dinner. I never showed you, but your boy knows his way around the kitchen."

"I 'ont know... You know what? What time is dinner?" I thought about turning him down, but what the hell? I was feeling depressed and needed to get out of the house.

"Dinner is at 7 P.M. sharp. That will give you some time to get all fancy. You know how you do," he chuckled.

"Okay. Text me the address, so I can put it in my GPS, and I'll see you at 7 P.M."

I laid back down on the bed, second-guessing myself. I grabbed the phone to cancel, but before I could press 'call', I hung the phone up. I took a quick shower and got dressed in a pair of slacks and a nice shirt. I applied a little face powder and lipstick and put my long mane into a bun. I kept it simple and classy.

As I pulled out of the driveway, I looked up and saw Devon looking out of the corner of the bedroom curtain. I cut the music up and sped off down the street. Christopher stayed over by The Village of Pelham, a nice, affluent neighborhood. The sizes of the houses were huge and looked like they were well cared for. *How does a PI afford this kind of living?* I thought as the GPS notified me that I had reached my destination. I made a right turn into the Victorian styled home. Before I could park, he walked out of the house, smiling from ear to ear. I parked and got out of the car. We exchanged hugs, and he walked into his house, and I followed.

Loving Him Ain't Worth A Damn Part 2

"Welcome to my home. Make yourself as comfortable as you want."

"This is nice, Christopher."

"Well, thank you, my love. The dining room is this way. I cooked lamb, potatoes, and asparagus."

"Wow! A man with taste. You never cease to amaze me at all."

"Well, when a man sees a woman that he wants, he will go out of his way to make sure she's comfortable at all times."

I just smiled because I was still in pain, but I couldn't let it show.

"Okay, I have gin, Jamaica Overproof Rum, and Baileys."

"Let me find out you've been studying me. Baileys is my favorite, so can I get a glass of that please?"

He placed a large bottle of Baileys in front of me, along with a bowl of ice. Soon after, dinner was served.

"I have to tell you that this is the most tender lamb I've ever eaten."

"Well, thank you. I was kind of nervous, but I seasoned it yesterday and let it marinate."

"Well, you did that, sir."

"Well, if you insist," he chuckled.

After dinner was over, we moved to the living room, where we watched a few movies. We drank some more and talked about growing up. Before you knew it, I was feeling myself. I knew I should've stopped drinking then, but I continued. This time, I switched to gin. I was hurting deep inside and needed something to numb the pain.

"Tell me, Christopher... you ever thought about killing someone?"

"Hmmm. I hope it's not me," he laughed.

"No, I'm serious. Has someone ever done something to you so bad that you just snapped and wanted to blow their fucking head off?"

"Well, no, but I felt like I wanted to kill my ex-wife. That woman dragged me through the mud. When she was done, I felt broken."

"Well, I did..."

"You did what?"

"I killed someone before."

"Ha ha, this gin is really taking a toll on you. Now you're telling fascinating stories."

"I'm serious. You know I told you my husband was killed. I killed him... That bastard cheated and cheated with everything that had a pussy, and I begged him and begged him to stop, but he laughed at me. He even told me one night that my pussy was too dry and the young bitches gave him life. How was I supposed to feel after that? My husband telling me that he wanted other bitches? I tell you what I did; I got me a gun, and I blew his fucking brains out. I bet you he ain't fucking nothing else now. That dick is dead!" I chuckled.

"Wow! That's a story there. Are you for real?"

Loving Him Ain't Worth A Damn Part 2

"Yes, I'm for real. See, Christopher, I keep telling you I'm not no little helpless woman. I know how to defend myself."

"I'm lost for words. So, how did you get away with it?"

"That was the easy part. I'd been planning his murder for about a year, so I created an alibi, and I made sure someone else found his body. When the police came, I almost fainted. I was so distraught with the death of my husband, I had to be hospitalized for days."

"And the gun?"

"No, no, I can't tell you all of that. If I do, I might have to kill you too."

"You're right. I don't want to end up like his ass. He's one unlucky fella. I just hope you were careful enough. You know there's no statute of limitation on murder."

"I ain't worried. Every so often, I call the station to see if there's any leads on the murder case of my husband, and each time, the detective on the case tells me there's still no news. Sometimes, I want to laugh out at how dumb they really are."

"Well, my love, on that note, let's drink to one of the smartest women of all times."

It felt good, getting that off of my chest. It had been years that I'd walked around with all of that bottled up inside. I took a big gulp of the gin. I cringed as it burned my stomach lining. I couldn't tell Christopher I was on the verge of murdering another sorry ass bastard.

Racquel Williams

"You're in no shape to drive home. So, either I drive you home or you spend the night in my guest room," Christopher said.

"Christopher, I'm not drunk, just a little tipsy," I said before I fell on the couch.

Loving Him Ain't Worth A Damn Part 2

CHAPTER EIGHT

Amoy

When it rained, it poured. I got an eviction notice today. I knew Devon's ass was being spiteful. His ass could've waited until I found somewhere else to live. What the fuck was I going to do? I applied for Section 8 a year ago, but the waiting list was long as fuck. I knew bitches that had been waiting for three years and still hadn't been approved yet. This stress was getting to be too damn much.

I thought about moving to the Bronx. At least those apartments were a tad bit cheaper, but they were way smaller. I had a few dollars saved up from working, but it wasn't enough for no two bedroom when I had to pay first, last, and security deposit.

***

We sat at the table, eating dinner. I tried to put on my best, but the stress of getting evicted was weighing heavily on me.

"Bae, what's going on wit' you? You seem a little distant. You good?"

I took a long sigh. I was trying to hide everything from him, but time was winding down, and I could no longer hide it.

"I'm getting put out of here."

"What you mean?" He gave me his full attention.

"I didn't tell you, but Devon was the one that got me this place. He told me he was paying the rent, so I wasn't wor…"

115

"What the fuck you mean you had this nigga paying for this and you have me over here? Man, what kind of foul shit you on?" he yelled.

"It wasn't like that. Once me and you started back fucking with each other, I wanted to move, but I didn't have the money."

"I ain't tryna hear that shit, B. You know damn well we ain't hurting for no paper. Yo, B, you on some sneaky shit, and I ain't feeling it. Yo, are you still fucking wit' that nigga?"

"No, I'm not. You know damn well what that nigga did to me. You must think I'm a weak bitch or something." I looked at him while the tears rolled down my face.

"Man, chill out wit' all that fucking crying. If we're together, you need to start being straight up with me. I can't take all these fucking secrets and shit."

"Ain't nobody keeping no damn secrets from you. It just slipped my mind."

"Well, fuck all that. You need to start looking for a new place ASAP."

"I don't have all the money to pay for everything."

"So, you ain't got a nigga to hold you down? Why you acting like this, Amoy?"

"Acting like what? I didn't know you were going to help. Lately, you seem a little distant and shit. I thought it was because we found out Jamal wasn't your son."

Loving Him Ain't Worth A Damn Part 2

"Man, you're tripping. I don't give a fuck if he's my blood or not. He's my fucking son. I'm the one he calls Dada, not that fuck nigga. And as far as me acting distant, B, you know what I do out here in these streets. I got fuck niggas tryna take my spot and the Feds tryna lock me up. My life ain't easy, B, but I love you, and I'm wit' you one hunnit. So, either you're in for this ride or you're not. I've got to know you wit' me all the way 'cause this shit can get real serious real quick."

He caught me off guard. I knew he was out there in these streets, but I never knew how deep he was. To be honest, I tried to stay out of his business. Now that he put me on the spot, I was sitting here, looking stupid as fuck.

"Listen, I love you with everything in me. I am grateful that God brought us back together, so I'm riding with you all the way."

"That's good to know 'cause I can't have no bitch around me that's not solid."

"You better watch yo motherfucking mouth. I ain't no bitch."

"My bad, but you know what I was tryna say. If you're on my team, you've got to be all the way solid."

"Yeah, I got you."

He reached into his pocket and pulled out a stack of cash. He started peeling off some money.

"Here, this is five stacks. It should be enough to find you a two-bedroom in a nice neighborhood. If you need more, let me know, and don't worry 'bout no furniture. We need new shit anyway."

"Awe, thank you, bae." I stood up and hugged him.

"Man, chill. You're my woman, and you should never want for anything."

I didn't say anything. I just smiled at him. I swear this dude was one of a kind. I just hoped this time he was serious about us and not just playing games.

"Aiight, I've got some things to handle. I'll hit you later."

"Okay. Love you, bae."

"Love you, B."

I locked the door behind him, feeling a lot better. I looked at the money I had in my hand. I could really get used to this type of treatment. Living the fast life, in the fast lane.

I heard a knock on the door. I ran over there and opened the door. I thought he had forgotten something.

"Yo, what's good?" The smile fell from my face and turned into one big frown.

"What the fuck you doing here?"

He pushed me out of the way and entered my house. I thought about running for my gun, but Marquise had taken it away, just in case the police ran up in here.

"You need to leave out of my shit now," I demanded.

Loving Him Ain't Worth A Damn Part 2

"Where my son at?"

"Why?" I folded my arms and gritted on him.

"Bitch, 'cause he's my motherfucking son. Do I need a reason to see him?"

"Get out of my shit with your disrespectful ass. If you want to see yo son, go ahead and file them court papers, so I can get some child support."

"Child support? So now yo silly ass wants to bring the white people up in our lives?"

"Ain't that what you did when you called CPS on me, talking 'bout I abuse my son?"

"What? Now you're making up shit. Bitch, I don't deal wit' the law. I'm a street nigga. Don't you ever disrespect me like that again."

"Boy, get out of my shit. Like I said, take me to court."

"Amoy, I'm telling you this and please take me seriously... If you or that fuck nigga ever tries to keep my seed away from me, I will bury both of y'all."

"You're a bitch ass nigga that only knows how to put your hands on a female. Trust me, Marquise ain't scared of you, and he showed you that before. You're weaker than me, nigga, and it shows in your eyes. I can't believe that I gave you the pussy. I should've bought me a strap and fucked you in the ass e'erynight."

"Bitch, fuck you." He balled his fist up.

"Yeah, go ahead, so they can lock yo ass up again."

"That's what you want. You know, at first I felt bad that I was fucking yo little sister, but now, I admit her pussy is way tighter and wetter than yours. Shit, you should consider having a threesome with us…"

"You're a lame ass nigga. Like I said, get your bitch ass out of my shit before I call the police on you. Don't forget; you still didn't get sentenced as of yet."

I walked over to the door and opened it as wide as I could. He gritted on me as he walked out. He stopped, grinned, and then said, "Bitch, I got you."

I didn't say shit to him. Instead, I just slammed the door shut in his face. That nigga was too old to be running around here acting like that. It hurt my heart that he was the father to my child because I prayed to God his dumbness didn't rub off on my child at all. If it was all up to me, he would not be allowed to be in his life, not acting like that.

Loving Him Ain't Worth A Damn Part 2

SHARI

I'd been wrestling with my thoughts for a few days. Part of me wanted to have an abortion, and the other part of me wanted to keep the baby. I knew Devon said he wasn't ready to have a baby right now, but truthfully, I wasn't trying to hear that shit. I felt like if this nigga fucked with me the way he claimed, then he would accept our child without giving a fuck who found out.

I took one last glance in the mirror. My stomach wasn't showing yet, but I could see that I was getting a bit thicker. The way the True Religion Jeans hugged my curves was definitely a good look. I knew one thing; if Mama didn't give me anything else in life, she gave me looks and a bad ass shape. I just prayed that, if I decided to have the baby, it wouldn't mess up my shape 'cause a bitch couldn't afford to have no grandma body.

I grabbed my purse and my phone and headed out the door. I exited my building and stepped on the pavement, getting ready to walk to my car.

"Yo, I was just coming to see you." I heard a male voice yell from behind me. I turned around quickly to see if the person was talking to me.

"Oh yeah, boo." I smiled when I realized it was DJ.

He didn't return the gesture. Instead, he approached me with a deadly grit on his face.

"Bitch, you fucking burned me," he yelled.

I quickly looked around to see if any of these nosey bitches were outside.

"Lower your voice. What are you talking about?" I acted like I had no idea what he was fussing about.

"Bitch, fuck you! Yo nasty ass done gave me a disease, knowing I had a fucking girl; now she done broke up with my ass."

"Boy, you better get the fuck on. You must've gotten that shit from one of yo hoes 'cause my shit ain't burning. I just went to the doctor, and I'm good. Matter-of-fact, I was going to call you to let you know we have a baby on the way."

"What, bitch? A fucking baby? That shit ain't mine," he yelled even louder.

By now, I saw a few bitches gathered on the steps, pretending like they were not there for the show.

"Well, I ain't goin' argue with you. Let's just see when the baby gets here."

He lunged towards me, grabbing my throat and pushing me into my parked car.

"Bitch, I just said it ain't mine." He pressed his gun against my temple.

"Get the fuck off me. You've lost your fucking mind. Do you see all these people out here?" I tried to talk some sense into him.

"Bitch, I don't give a fuck. I'll blow your fucking brains out all over this fucking street. You fucked my life up; my fucking bitch left me, and now you're talkin' 'bout you're pregnant. Hoe, I ain't got shit to live for," he yelled.

You could hear the anger in that nigga's voice, and I could feel the pressure on my neck. Tears started rolling down my face as I didn't know if I wanted him to hurry up and use the gun... that way, I wouldn't suffer like this.

I heard a car approaching and started praying that one of these nosey bitches had called the police. I waited a few seconds, but my hope faded when I didn't hear anything else.

A few minutes later, I heard a voice yell, "Yo, what the fuck you doing?"

"What you say, nigga? You better mind yo motherfucking business."

"This my bitch right here, so this is my motherfucking business, nigga. Matter-of-fact, take your hands off her," Devon demanded.

I didn't know if I should be happy that he was here or wish I was dead because of what he might find out.

DJ took his hand from around my throat and aimed his gun at Devon. I lifted my head up and realized Devon was aiming a gun at that nigga also.

"Nigga, who the fuck are you? I'm out here handling this bitch 'cause I fucked that bitch and she burned me."

"You fucked her?" Devon quizzed.

"Yeah, this hoe hit me up about a week and a half ago. She wanted me to come over and fuck. My dumb ass, not thinking anything about it, came through. Now my girl went to the doctor and she got gonorrhea."

"Yo, you was fucking this nigga, B?"

"He's lying. He's just mad that he tried to fuck, and I turned him down. Matter-of-fact, I told him that I have a nigga, and that nigga said fuck you."

"Yo, nigga, it's all good if you're wifeing this hoe. This bitch been a thot since junior high school, fucking and sucking e'ery nigga that had a few dollars. I'm just stupid as fuck, running up in her ass without using rubbers."

I could see the anger plastered across Devon's face. "Baby, please don't believe him. If I had anything, I would've given it to you. I swear he's just trying to break us up," I said to Devon while I started crying. I was desperate and didn't give a fuck if these bitches and niggas were staring.

"Yo, son, if you want to trust this hoe, it's on you. I'm out though. Bitch, you're lucky. I'ma catch you though." He tucked his gun in his waist and walked off.

I looked at Devon as he walked off. I grabbed his arm. "Babe, please don't believe him. I swear that nigga's lying."

"Yo, let's go." He started walking up the stairs.

Loving Him Ain't Worth A Damn Part 2

I dreaded going into the apartment with him, but what choice did I have? I couldn't afford to let him go, knowing he might not come back. I nervously tried to open the door. The key fumbled in my hand. I tried again, and this time, the door unlocked. He entered first, and I cautiously stepped in.

"So, you're out here fucking niggas and shit." He grabbed me by my weave from behind.

"Devon, I swear that nigga's lying on me. I never fucked him, and I damn sure didn't give him no damn STD."

"Bitch, you're a fucking liar. Kennedy's ass has the same fucking thing, and guess who the fucking common denominator bitch is? You."

He took my head and pushed it into the wall. "Noooo," I screamed out in anguish.

"Bitch, who the fuck you think I am?"

"You just broke my nose," I cried.

I put my hand to my face and felt the sticky substance, which I concluded was blood. He wasn't done though; he dragged me by my weave and pushed me on the sofa. He then pointed his gun in my face.

"You're a nasty hoe; you know that? So, who the fuck you pregnant for, this nigga?"

"I swear I never fucked him. This is your baby," I cried.

"Bitch, I told yo ass to get a fucking abortion. You thought I was playing? I don't want that shit, and I don't want yo trifling ass no more either."

"Please don't say that! Devon, I love you. I swear on my mama's soul, I never fucked him. He's lying, babe." I tried getting up.

"Sit yo' ass down, hoe. I should've known you were trifling as fuck when you still wanted me after you knew I was fucking with yo sister."

"Devon, baby, please. You don't mean all this. This is me, yo baby girl. You promised to never leave me."

"Man, fuck you, bitch. I should shoot yo ass, but I ain't goin' waste no bullet on yo ass. Lose my motherfucking number, bitch."

He hawked up some spit and spit dead between my eyes. "I wish you die, bitch."

He started to walk off, and I jumped off the couch, diving on the ground and holding on to his legs. "Please don't leave me, Devon."

"Get the fuck off me, bitch." He tried kicking me.

I held on tightly, like my life depended on it. "Devon, I love you. I swear I'll do anything for you. I swear anything."

He stood still for a minute. "Anything?"

"Yes, anything."

"Suck this dick for me." I really thought this nigga was playing… that was until I looked up and noticed he had taken his dick out of the grey sweat pants that he was wearing. I looked at him for confirmation.

"Bitch, what are you looking at? You said you'd do anything. Fuck it then. I'm out."

"No, I'll do it," I said as I grabbed his dick.

I started licking the tip of his dick, but I almost gagged because I could tell he didn't bathe. His dick smelled like purse sweat and stale pussy. I tried not to smell it and just started sucking. This was the most humiliating shit, but I had to show him how much I wanted him. I massaged his balls while I sucked his dick. To be honest, my happiness depended on it, and those were the only thoughts that I had to help me get through this. I sucked harder and used my hands to massage his balls more aggressively, trying to speed up the process, silently begging God to make him cum.

"Aargh, damn. Yeah, right there," he said as he grabbed my head and pulled it in towards him.

I just breathed harder and sucked. Within minutes, he was exploding. I tried to jump back, but he had a strong hold on my head.

"Where you going, bitch? Swallow this cum."

There was no escaping, so I swallowed the cum. I used my tongue and licked it up. After I was finished, I ran to the bathroom, put my head in the toilet bowl, and vomited everything up. I tried to get up, but I still had to vomit up the breakfast that I ate earlier. I was sick to my stomach and had no energy left in my body. I took a seat by the toilet bowl and rested my head on the rim. Tears rolled down my face. I'd never felt this low in my life and to think it was by the hands of the man that was supposed to love me.

I waited patiently to see if he was going to come check on me, but about ten minutes later, I realized that wasn't going to happen. I thought he was just sitting out there, trying to get his mind right. I got up, brushed my teeth, and rinsed with some mouthwash. I was trying to get rid of that bitter taste that came from his cum. I then walked out in the living room. I soon discovered that he was nowhere in sight, and my house door was wide open. I ran over to the door and looked in the hallway, but there was no one around. I walked back inside, slammed the door, and ran to the window to see if his car was still out there, but it was gone. I walked back over to the couch and grabbed my phone out of my purse. I called his number, but it went straight to voicemail. Ten tries later and the same thing was happening. I threw the phone across the room, shattering it. "Damn you, Devon. I did what you wanted," I screamed out in mental anguish.

I ran to the fridge, grabbed a beer, and started drinking. *I swear I can't live without him,* I thought as I gulped the alcohol down.

Loving Him Ain't Worth A Damn Part 2

KENNEDY

This was strange; I tried calling Christopher two days ago, and he had not answered or returned my calls. That was so out of character for him. At first, I charged it to him being busy working on a new case, but I checked my phone and he still had not called last night. Hmm, I hoped my friend was okay and hadn't gotten himself in a dangerous situation.

I went ahead about my business, taking care of some errands and grabbing a few things out of the grocery store. I was pulling in my driveway when I noticed a black SUV following closely behind. It slowed down after it got to my gate and then it pulled off. That seemed a little suspicious, but I blew it off. I proceeded to take the things out of the car.

***

"Babes, I need to talk to you real quick." Devon startled me when he walked into my room.

"What is it?"

He took a seat on the edge of the bed. He looked like a man with the world on his shoulders.

"You know how, years ago, we talked about adopting a child?"

"Hmm, that was before I knew you were slinging your dick around town."

"I know that, but just hear me out. I know I've been telling you that the baby that girl has ain't mine, but I need to come clean with you. I think he's mine."

"So, what the fuck you telling me that for? Isn't that supposed to be between you and your bitch?"

"Kennedy, please stop! This is not easy, but I need your support on this."

I looked at that nigga like he was a fool. Did I hear him mention 'support'?

"Listen, you're wasting your fucking time, talking to me about a fucking monkey that you made while cheating on me. I have no desire nor would I ever help you or that bastard," I said in a high pitched tone.

"I ain't asking you for no money. I've got my own shit. All I'm saying is that the bitch ain't in no position to take care of my seed, and I want to take my son from her. I was only asking you if he can come live with us for a little while."

I stood up immediately and looked at this nigga to see if he was really serious about what the fuck he just said out of his mouth. "You must have fallen down and knocked your fucking head… You think I would allow you to bring your little bastard in my house? How dare you even think about it, much less have the balls to approach me with such bullshit? You're barely living here your damn self."

Loving Him Ain't Worth A Damn Part 2

"Damn, I guess our wedding vows didn't mean anything to you. We're supposed to be there for each other, no matter what the situation. What happened to you weathering the storm with me? I know I fell short of being the man that you want, but I've changed, but you don't give a nigga no credit. Kennedy, it's me, the man that you fell for. How can you say you fuck with me one hundred but you're not willing to accept my seed?"

"That speech sounded convincing and everything, but I was never a weak bitch, and I'm too fucking old to be yo fool. You made that bastard; you chose the bitch. It's your mess, so you clean it up on your fucking own."

He looked at me as if he was shocked. I didn't pay him no fucking mind. Instead, I picked up the remote and turned the television on, trying my hardest to tune him out.

CHAPTER NINE

Amoy

After searching for weeks, I finally found a two bedroom over on Thirteen Avenue. It was really nice, and the landlord seemed like someone that I could get along with. I had two weeks before the court date, so I was trying to be gone before then.

Getting the place was one thing but packing was another. Jamal's things were top priority, so I made sure those were packed first. Marquise insisted that I leave all of the old furniture and shop for new stuff for the new apartment. He didn't say it in too many words, but I think he didn't want anything that had to do with Devon. That was fine with me because I needed a new couch and a new dining room set.

I made sure everything was washed and folded neatly, so I wouldn't have too much to do once we moved. I was on my last load of clothes when I heard a knock at the door. I peeped out the hole and realized it was two uniformed police officers. My heart suddenly dropped because the first thing that popped in my mind was DFACS. I stood there, wondering if I should open the door or not. I heard a couple more knocks, and then I opened the door.

"Yes, may I help you?"

"Ma'am, are you Amoy Simpson?"

"Yes, I am," I reluctantly said.

"I'm afraid that I have some bad news."

Loving Him Ain't Worth A Damn Part 2

I looked at their faces, trying to figure out what the fuck they were talking about.

"Your mother was murdered this morning by her live in boyfriend."

I looked at him, expressionless, and I had to catch myself real fast.

"Ma'am, did you hear us? Your mother was killed this morning by her live in boyfriend. You're listed as her next of kin."

"Yeah, I heard you."

"We already have him in custody and have a full confession from him. It seems like he and your mother were fighting over drugs and money. He grabbed a knife and stabbed her in the abdomen. He did call the ambulance, but she died on her way to the hospital."

"Right now, she's at the coroner's office. We would like for you to come down and identify her body."

"Umm, you might want to hit my little sister up. She can identify her."

They both turned their heads, looking at me as if they were shocked at what I'd just said to them. Shit, if they only knew how that bitch treated me, then they wouldn't be too surprised at the statement that I'd just made.

"You're the next of kin listed."

"Look, no disrespect, but let me get my sister's number, and she can help y'all out," I snapped.

I turned to go back in. I grabbed my phone and gave them the number. I was ready for them to get the fuck on.

"Thank you, ma'am, and again, our condolences."

I smiled at them, waited for them to walk off, and then I slammed the door. I stood in the middle of my floor, just staring at the walls. I was feeling kind of confused.

***

It had been three days since I found out my mama was killed by the same old nasty ass nigga that used to molest me, and from what Shari's lying ass said, he used to molest her also. When I first heard she was dead, to be honest, I really didn't give a fuck. My whole life, she treated me like I was the scum of the earth. Our last words the other day were very disrespectful, but I never expected to hear that she was gone and definitely not murdered. Last night, I laid in bed, thinking about her and how she once was when I was a young child. She wasn't all that mean before the nigga and the drugs. Tears flowed on my pillow as reality set in that I never knew my daddy, and now the woman that gave birth to me was gone also.

"Baby, did you talk to your sister?" Marquise asked as he walked into the room.

"Nah, why would I talk to that bitch?" I threw the clothes I was folding down and turned my full attention to him.

Loving Him Ain't Worth A Damn Part 2

"I mean, y'all mama just passed, and from what you tell me, it's only the two of you. Now might be a good time to mend y'all relationship."

"Listen, baby, I love you, and I respect you, but don't you ever tell me that I need to mend anything with that bitch. I didn't do anything to her ass. That bitch is jealous of me for no damn reason. I have never done one damn thing to her ass."

"B, I know, but yo mama gone, and you're the big sister. I'm pretty sure y'all both in pain."

"What time you getting in later?" I quizzed, changing the conversation.

"It'll be after midnight. Why, what's good?"

"Nothing, just want to go to this furniture place over by Baychester Avenue."

"Yeah, I did forget. What time you tryna go?"

"I have three heads to braid today, and then I'm done for the day. I'll call you before I finish, so we can meet up."

"Aiight, cool. Just lemme know." He kissed me on the cheek and then walked out of the door.

He wasn't gone a full minute when I sat on the couch. Mama's face flashed across my eyes. Tears welled up in my eyes. I felt an emptiness in the bottom of my heart. This was the first time I felt this hurt over her death. I clenched the pillow that was on the couch and buried my head in it. I cried, not caring how mad I was at her. I swear,

Racquel Williams

I wished I could take back those horrible words that I said to her weeks ago. Just one more chance to let her know I loved her. I was caught up in different emotions. I loved her... nah, I hated her for the way she treated me. I felt so alone and cold, like an abandoned child that was yearning for her mother's love. Only it was too late for all that...

***

This wasn't a good day. I was at the funeral parlor, making final arrangement for my mother. "What the fuck you think you're doing? You know damn well Mama didn't want to get cremated," my stupid ass sister yelled as we both stood at the morgue.

"You need to lower your voice. Furthermore, she's dead and has no say in this. If I'm correct, she didn't leave a dollar to help with these expenses. I see you running your big ass mouth, but I don't see you trying to chip in with a dollar. It's all on me, the one she despises. You were her pet and should be handling this shit."

"Bitch, whatever. You jumped yo ass over here, making plans and shit, and now you want to complain about somebody helping you. Nah, put your big girl panties on and make it happen." She grinned in my face.

"I'm done entertaining you, little bitch. She will be cremated and that's final."

I shot her ass a dirty look and walked off. This wasn't the time to deal with her little ungrateful behind.

Loving Him Ain't Worth A Damn Part 2

I planned a small ceremony at the parlor because she didn't belong to any church. I invited a few people that I knew she was close to in Mount Vernon, but only a handful showed up. Marquise and I sat on one side while Shari sat on the next. It was a shame the way Mama lived her life, burning bridges behind her and never making amends before she died. After the funeral, I took the urn and brought it home. I placed it in a box and put it in the closet.

"Babe, you okay?" Marquise walked up behind me.

"Yes. Just a little hurt, you know?"

"Look, regardless of what she did to you, or how she treated you, truth is, she's still yo mama. I mean, I can't imagine losing mine."

"You know I really appreciate you stepping in and taking care of the bill. I don't know what I would do without you these past couple of months. You've really been my rock."

"Nah, B. It's the other way 'round. You kno' I just be out here, living reckless and shit, not giving a fuck, but the minute that we started fucking with each other again, it's like I have a whole different look on life. I love you, B, and we're in this for life."

"Awe, babe, I'm happy that you feel this way. I love you so much, and I'm happy that God gave us another chance."

His phone started ringing, and he looked down at it. "Damn, bae, you goin' be aiight? I've got a run to make in Queens."

"Yeah, I'm good. Gonna lay down for a little bit before I pick up Jamal from daycare."

"Listen, B, we're in this together. You hear me?" He stared in my eyes.

"Yeah, I hear you, boo." I smiled, so he could know that I was with him one hundred percent.

"Aiight, bae. I love you. I'm out."

Before I could respond, he was out the door. I smiled as I thought about our relationship and the bond we shared. I didn't believe in fairytales, but this one was one for the books.

POP! POP! POP!

I thought I heard gunshots or was I tripping? I ran over to my window and looked outside.

"No, help. Somebody just got shot," I heard somebody yell.

I grabbed my phone and dialed Marquise's number, but there was no response. I dashed out the door, and before I could run down the steps, I noticed the clothing. It was the same outfit that Marquise was wearing. I dashed through the crowd that was formed.

"Noooooo, baby, nooooooo. Call an ambulance please."

My baby was on the ground with two gunshot wounds in his chest. He was bleeding heavily. I gently lifted his head off the concrete and placed it on my leg. I noticed the gun in his hand. I thought about taking it and hiding it real quick. I took a quick glance around me and realized that was a very bad idea.

"Does anybody know CPR?" I yelled.

Loving Him Ain't Worth A Damn Part 2

"I'm a registered nurse," an older lady said and walked over to him.

I moved out of her way, and she started working on him.

"No, God, no. Did y'all see who did this?" I turned around and asked no one in particular. No one said anything. Instead, everyone was whispering or talking on their phones.

I heard the sirens and felt a little better. "Y'all move out the way," an EMT worker said as he dashed through with a stretcher.

I trembled as I watched them place him on the gurney and hurriedly put him in the ambulance.

"Can I ride with him please? I'm his girl."

"Sure, let's go."

I watched in despair as they tried their best to keep him alive.

"God, pleaseeeee don't take my baby away," I pleaded.

When the ambulance reached the hospital, I jumped out of the back and stood to the side. I saw a team of doctors rush to the ambulance, and they took him inside. I knew he was in critical condition by the way they were behaving. I ran into the hospital and tried to follow them.

"Ma'am, you're not allowed to go back there," a doctor informed me.

"Why not? That's my baby." I shot him a desperate look.

"Only doctors and the nurses are allowed in the OR. He's in critical condition and needs immediate care."

I saw there was no use in debating, so I took one last look in the direction that they took him and walked off. I walked into the waiting room and found a seat in the corner. I sat down, hanging my head in my lap. My heart was ripped apart as I constantly talked to God.

My cell phone started ringing. *I wonder who the fuck would be calling me at a time like this,* I thought.

"Hellooo," I answered with major attitude.

"Miss Simpson, this is Miss James from Brighter Ones Daycare. You were supposed to pick Jamal up about twenty minutes ago."

"Shit. Umm, I'm so sorry."

"Is something the matter, Miss Simpson?"

"My boyfriend got shot, and I'm at the hospital with him. I'm so sorry. I'm…"

"Oh, my. Sorry to hear that. Is he going to be alright?"

"No, he's in surgery right now. It doesn't look good." I broke down crying again.

"You know what? I'm going to be here until about seven. Go ahead and see about your boyfriend. I've got the baby."

"Are you sure 'cause I can be there in about twenty-five minutes?"

"Yes, I'm sure. I've got him. Now get off the phone and go handle your business."

"Yes, ma'am."

Loving Him Ain't Worth A Damn Part 2

I cracked a smile because of her in control attitude. She had always been warm but stern.

Seconds turned into minutes, and minutes turned into hours. I paced the emergency room floor and kept asking the nurse questions. The bitch acted like she was irritated, but oh well.

I was about to sit down when I saw his sister walk in, along with two other chicks that I didn't recognize. She walked up to the counter and briefly spoke with the nurse. As soon as she walked off, I approached her. "Hey, Sonja, I don't know if you remember me..."

"Yeah, I remember you. What happened to my brother? Who tried to kill him?" she asked between sobs.

"I don't know. He told me he had a run to make. He left out the door, and a few seconds later, I heard gunshots. I tried calling him, but when he didn't respond, I ran out there. That's when I realized it was him on the ground." Tears welled up in my eyes as I relived the emotions that I felt coming out of the door.

"Man, I swear my brother don't be fucking with these niggas. They better pray that he ain't seen whoever did it 'cause it's goin' be bloodshed e'erywhere," she cried.

"Come on, Sonja. Come sit down, babes," one of the chicks, that I assumed was her friend or family member, said.

As they walked off, the other chick stayed behind. "So you're the bitch that Marquise was creeping with?"

"Creeping with? You mean we live together, and by the way, who the fuck are you?" I asked, bracing myself for the inevitable.

"Say what, hoe? He don't live wit' yo ass. He lives with me and his daughter."

His sister must've caught wind of what was taking place because she bolted to where we were standing. "Really, Kaye... my motherfucking brother is in there, fighting for his life, and you're in here worried about who he's fucking with?"

"Girl, this bitch knows she ain't got no business being up here. E'erybody knows that I'm his bitch and ain't going nowhere."

"You're a silly bitch. I told yo ass not to come up here 'cause I know you ain't got no chill. If my brother don't make it, ain't nobody going to be getting no dick. So if y'all can't keep the drama down, y'all can fucking leave."

"I'm straight." I shrugged.

I didn't wait for a response; I walked off. I thought about smoking a Black and Mild. Shit, I realized I didn't have my purse. My head was pounding, and my anger was elevated. This bitch had the nerve to add to what I was already going through. I wasn't worried about who he was fucking. My first concern was if he was going to make it.

I waited and waited, and there was still no word on how his surgery was coming along. I looked at the time, and it was steadily approaching 7 P.M. I had no choice. I walked out and headed to my car. I was tripping; my car was at home. I pulled up the Uber app and request a cab. On my way to the daycare, I prayed and cried. I just wanted to grab my son and make it back to the hospital.

After I grabbed Jamal, I rushed to the house, grabbed my car, and sped off. I stopped at McDonald's, grabbed him a kid's meal, and then headed straight back to Mount Vernon Hospital. I parked and picked my baby up. I rushed into the hospital, hoping that I would get some good news. I walked over to his sister, but she was still waiting.

***

I must've dozed off because I felt a slight tap on my shoulder. I jumped up immediately.

"Sorry, but my brother's out of surgery. I think you might want to see him."

I stood up and followed her. She kind of gave me a run-down of what was going on. When we reached the room, I was kind of scared to step in because I wasn't sure what to expect.

"Let me keep your son out here while you go in. He doesn't need to see his father like this," the nurse said.

"Thank you." I was going to correct her, about him not being Jamal's father, but she was right. That was his daddy.

I also noticed that there were two uniformed police sitting outside of his room. I knew then that they were going to charge Marquise with that gun once he recovered.

I pulled up my big girl panties and walked in the room. I stood there, and he had wires coming from everywhere. He was purple in complexion, and his face was swollen. I leaned over and touched his hand. I really didn't know what to say. "Babe, I swear we goin' get through this," I whispered.

"Listen, did the police come talk to you?" Sonja asked.

"Nah, only when we were at the complex."

"They better find out who the fuck did this to him."

My mind started wondering. That was when it dawned on me that he was in the streets heavily, and this could be a beef. The only thing was that he never mentioned that he had any kind of beef going on.

After I stayed there for a while, I realized that it was time to get my son home. At times like these, I wished that I had some type of help. "Aye, babes, I've got to go get my baby home. Please take my number and call me if there's any change. I'll be back tomorrow morning, as soon as I drop him off at daycare."

"Okay. Our mom is on her way up here from Atlanta."

We hugged, and I left out. The one lady was still in the room with Sonja when I left, but I noticed the bitch that claimed she was Marquise's girl was nowhere to be found. I wiped my tears as I stepped on the elevator. I hated to leave him like this, but I had no choice.

I got downstairs and stepped off the elevator. I looked around to see if I saw the bitch anywhere, but she wasn't. I figured she was somewhere moping around. These bitches were silly as fuck, always running up on a bitch. Shit, her best bet was to wait to confront that nigga because I wasn't going anywhere.

I stopped by Burger King to grab me some nuggets, I was mentally and physically drained and had no intentions of cooking tonight. I pulled up at the apartment complex. My heart was heavy. I sat in the car for a few minutes, trying to gather my thoughts before I exited the vehicle. Jamal was sleeping, so I picked him up and carried him inside.

After I put him in the bed, I sat on the couch. I needed to take a shower, but I wasn't moving. My mind was on Marquise. I hoped he understood that I wanted to be there with him so badly, but I had no one to watch my son. I attempted to eat one of the nuggets, but I couldn't even chew it. I spit it out and threw the bag away. I was about to pour a glass of wine when I heard a knock on my door. I got up to see who it was. It was the police.

"Damn, were they watching my shit?" I said before I opened the door.

"Miss Simpson?"

"Yes, what's going on?"

"We want to talk to you about a shooting that took place out here earlier. It's our understanding that the gentleman was a close friend of yours, and he was just leaving your apartment."

"I don't know what to tell y'all. Yes, he's my boyfriend, and he left. Other than that, I don't know anything else."

"Well, do you know why he had a gun?"

"I never saw him with a gun before, so I wouldn't know."

"Miss Simpson, we're only trying to find out who's responsible for this crime. If you're holding back information…"

I cut his ass off. "Listen, it's been a long day. I don't know anything." I didn't wait for them to respond. Instead, I shot them a fake smile and then closed my door. I wasn't stupid. I knew they had run a background check on him, and they also knew that he was a convicted felon with a gun. I knew it was only a matter of time before they arrested him on gun charges. My plan for tomorrow morning was to find him a lawyer.

I was just about to jump in the shower when I heard another bang on my door. *Man, if these motherfuckers don't get the fuck on…* I was ready to curse these motherfucking police out.

"Yo, I just told y'all…"

It wasn't the police but my nosey ass neighbor that lived downstairs. "Oh, what do you want?" I was ready to slam the door in her face too. This bitch was knocking on my door like we were cool or something.

"Girl, I just came to see how ole boy was doing. I heard the shots out of my bedroom window."

"He's good. Now I'm tired and need to take a shower." I was about to lock the door.

"I think I saw who shot him."

Loving Him Ain't Worth A Damn Part 2

I turned back around quickly. This bitch had my full attention and better not be playing either.

"You saw who did it?"

"Well, not exactly, but minutes before your boyfriend came out, I saw a black car pull into the parking lot. My nosey ass was trying to see who came out of the car, but the person remained inside. Then, as soon as the shots rang out, I watched the vehicle slowly pull off from beside your boyfriend."

"What kind of car?"

"I'm not good with cars, but I'm almost sure it looked like a Chrysler 300."

I almost fainted when she said what model car it was.

"Are you okay? Do you know who drives that car?"

"Huh, say what? Nah, I don't. I just feel sick. Must be 'cause I ain't eat all day. Did you tell the police what you just told me?"

"You know I don't fuck with the law. Shit, they killed my brother a few years ago, talkin' 'bout he was trying to run them over."

"Listen, I'm sorry to hear about your brother, but I need to make some tea or something. My stomach is killing me."

"Okay, sure. Keep me posted on ole boy's health."

"I got you," I lied.

I locked the door and leaned my face up against it. This couldn't be; there was no way.

I walked to the couch and grabbed my phone. I dialed Devon's number.

"Yo!"

"Where were you earlier?"

"Man, what kind of question is that? You ain't my bitch."

"I swear if you had anything to do with Marquise's shooting, you're gonna pay."

"Yo, bitch you're tripping. I ain't shoot nobody. Matter-of-fact, don't call my phone accusing me of shit."

Before I could respond, he hung up. I had a bad feeling about him. All the threats he made popped up in my head, especially the last time that I saw him. I thought about calling the police to let them know, but I had no proof, only what the neighbor told me. Hmm, I needed to think.

Loving Him Ain't Worth A Damn Part 2

KENNEDY

Some might say I'd lost my got damn mind, and I probably did. Weeks after Devon kept begging me to let his little bastard stay here, I finally gave in and told him it was okay if and when he got custody. The one thing I couldn't agree to, though, was me lying on that girl. Don't get me wrong, I didn't give a fuck about that little bitch, and if you asked me, she deserved everything that she has coming to her. See, these little bitches had to start realizing that not all these sweet stories that these niggas fed them were true. A nigga was going to say whatever the fuck they wanted to say to get into those drawers and get to the pussy. But it was up to them not to fall for the foolery. I knew what it was though; a lot of them thought they were getting over on the next woman. Wrong. What that nigga did to his main bitch, he'd end up doing twice as worse to the bitch on the side. Oh well, fuck them all. All of this would soon be over.

I dried my hands and hurried up and grabbed my cell phone. I took a quick glance at the screen. I smiled as I answered quickly. "Hello there, stranger."

"Hey there, beautiful."

"Christopher, where the hell have you been? I haven't heard from you since the night that I left your house. I've called, texted, and I was tempted to stop by your house."

"Just been tied up doing some work. I had a case that required my undivided attention."

"Well, you could've shot me a text or something, you know?"

"You're right. Listen, I'll make it up to you."

"Hmmm, you better make it soon. I've been doing a lot of thinking lately. I might not be in NY much longer."

"You're moving? Where are you going?" he shouted.

"I've been thinking about moving to Florida with my sister. I think I've mentioned her to you before."

"Yes, sure. I just didn't think y'all were that close."

"We're not close, but that's my only relative, plus I need a change of scenery. There's nothing really in New York for me."

"You taking the husband with you?"

"Ha ha, no way. I am going by myself."

"Oh okay. Well, Miss Lady, you know if you want me to go with you, all you have to do is say the word."

"Ha ha, there's no way I could possibly ask you to pack up your life and leave. Plus, I need to take time to myself. I need to refocus on my life. Travel the world a bit and just live life a little."

"Well, promise me you'll keep in touch, and I would love to see you before you leave, if you don't mind."

"Well, my plan is not concrete yet. I'm in the planning stage, but I'll keep you posted."

"Okay, my love. Talk to you later."

I put the phone back down on the counter and went back to cutting my greens. I planned on cooking Sunday dinner tomorrow. Something

Loving Him Ain't Worth A Damn Part 2

ran across my mind as I stood at the sink, chopping away. Something about Christopher had changed. I didn't know what was, but right after that night when I poured out my soul about my deceased husband, I noticed he was rarely around. Let me remind you that this was a man that I could barely keep away, but nowadays, I couldn't seem to find him. The thought of him betraying me ran across my mind... What if he told the police about my confession? Nonsense. If he did, they would've kicked my door in already. So, what was so different about Christopher? Maybe he found a new love. "Ha ha, Christopher, you dirty old man," I chuckled as I washed the greens in salt water.

"Did I hear you talking to yourself, my love?"

"Oh, my mother once told me it's okay to talk to one's self as long as you didn't respond to one's self."

"Well, Mother was a wise woman. So, what are you cooking?"

"Nothing, my dear. I was seasoning up some greens for Sunday dinner."

"I had a long day, babe, so I handled all my business early, so I can spend quality time with you. I brought dinner home," he said, followed by his sexy, make my pussy wet, smile.

"Is that so? You really are a changed man. A girl could get used to this kind of treatment again."

"This is nothing, my love. I told you that once you gave me another chance, I would make you the happiest woman in the world."

I felt like throwing up, but instead, I smiled like a young schoolgirl crushing on her new lover. Truth was, Devon was a slime ball that would do whatever it took to weasel his ass back into my life.

"Dinner was delicious," I said to him as he cleaned up and packed away our leftovers.

"I've got somebody even better for your dessert." He winked at me and smiled.

"Well, on that note, let me go take a shower." I winked back at him. I rubbed his hand as I walked off.

I had no idea how long I was going to be able to play this doting wife. I knew I needed to put my plans into motion fast if I planned on getting this no good ass bastard out of my life.

As soon as I stepped out of the shower, Devon was standing there, naked, dick hanging like he'd been in an African Mandingo tribe or something. Yes, I said it; y'all know how them Africans be dancing in the wilderness with those long cones covering up the goodies. LOL, an inside joke. I giggled to myself.

I grabbed my Bath and Body Works, Sex on the Platter, lotion. As I was bent over, lotioning my legs, I felt Devon's strong hands rubbing my ass.

"Damn, babe, you're making me horny as fuck." He stood in front of me, massaging his dick.

Loving Him Ain't Worth A Damn Part 2

I couldn't say anything; he picked me up and carried me over to the bed. He bent my ass over, revealing pussy in the back. Devon ran his soft lips on my back, slightly up from my hips.

"I miss you so much, baby." He continued kissing on my lower back.

Damn, his lips felt so soothing caressing my back, I held back my words until his tongue slithered between the crack of my ass. "Hmmmm." I let out some air and squeezed my ass tight. His warm slobber hit the crack of my ass; I braced myself because his tongue slid into my hole.

"Oooo, ahhh," I hissed in between moans. Dammit, man; this shit was feeling so great. I struggled to keep my eyes open; they were slightly closed.

Devon spread my ass wide and licked my ass as if he was licking the cake mix out of the bowl. My pussy was dripping wet. I stuck two fingers inside my pussy and worked in and out slowly.

"Ohhhh, oooo, shit, yes." I couldn't hold back. Juice started leaking and flowing onto my fingers. I had to taste myself. Just as I thought, I tasted like passion fruit, since that was all I inserted into my body.

"Stay just like that, babe." Devon wrapped his arms around my waist and pulled me closer to him. He eased his head inside the house before thrusting his way in. "Just like that, babe." He took long and

153

hard strokes, scraping my walls. His dick was touching my entire insides.

"Yesss. Fuck me, my king." I begged.

I was feeling good. I wanted to feel his dick ripping my insides out. I loved when he took long and gentle strokes; each thrust felt like I was losing my breath because he was really into it.

Shit was getting intense. He pulled my hair with one hand and held onto my chin with the other hand. "Mmmmm." The pain was devastating... The ripping I was talking about... let's say I felt his dick touching my stomach. "Yes, Devon. Oh, shit, I love this dick." I bit down on his fingers and bounced my ass on his dick. "I love this dick,'" I yelled, taking every inch of him.

Devon removed his wet fingers from my mouth but still kept his left hand wrapped around my hair, pulling it.

I felt four fingers graze across my lower back, and then I felt his thumb jam into my ass.

"Auhhh, shit. Jesus take the wheel," I cried out. His thumb and dick were working magic at the same time. I couldn't stop creaming on his dick and thumb. I knew this nigga was a freak, but goddamn, he was trying to turn me the fuck out, and I was loving every bit of it.

After busting my last nut, my knees buckled underneath me, I flopped onto my stomach. Devon braced both hands on my lower back and pounded my ass out until he nutted inside my goodies. Minutes later, he collapsed on top of me. We were both gasping for air and enjoying each other's company, lost in our own world, reminiscing about what just went down.

After I caught my breath and got my head leveled, I got up. I walked back to the bathroom and washed off real quick. I was definitely a fool for a good fuck. This was one of the best fucks that Devon had ever given me, and since he wouldn't be around for long, I might as well enjoy them while it lasted.

Racquel Williams

SHARI

Blowing up the phone
Hope she see me calling her.
I whip up in the driveway,
She done packed up all my stuff.
And I'm like, what the fuck?
Can't even talk to her
Ain't gone lie
This pussy good
It make me feel like stalking her.
We supposed to be in love
We 'posed to be in love
We supposed to be in love
Til it ain't no breaking up
We supposed to be in love
Til it ain't no breaking up

I sat on the floor, playing Kevin Gates' song over and over while dialing Devon's number over and over. There was no response.

How could he be this cold to me? I'd just lost my mother and not once did he call me to say he was sorry. How could he do this to me? The woman that he loved? I turned against my sister for him. I couldn't stop the tears from flowing. I picked up the phone to call my mama and quickly realized she was no longer with me. She was gone... Mama was my world. My everything. God, how was I supposed to live without her? "God, answer me? How can you say you love me but take away the only person that I love?" I put the bottle of Cîroc Vodka Peach to my head and couldn't stop drinking.

Twenty minutes later, I was drunk and high as fuck, but instead of feeling much better, I was still feeling lonely and angry. I gargled with mouthwash, sprayed my body, and grabbed my car keys and got into my car. I shouldn't be driving, but fuck it. I didn't have nothing to live for anyway. My best friend was gone, and it wouldn't be a bad idea for me to join her.

I made my way to my sister's apartment. Shit, I hadn't seen the bitch since the day of Mama's wake, and even then, she was still acting like a bitch towards me. I mean, I knew I fucked her nigga, but shit, she should be thanking me. I did get his cheating ass away from her. At least she wasn't the one he was cheating on right now. I wiped the tear that fell on my face.

"Bitch, quit all this fucking crying. I didn't raise no weak ass bitch." Surprisingly, I heard Mama's voice in my head. I almost crashed when I heard that because this was the first time, since she died, that I had heard her voice.

"Mama, is that you?" I looked over to the seat across from me. I didn't see her. I glanced in my mirror, to the backseat, and didn't see her. "C'mon, answer me, Mama. I need you. How you gonna say some shit to me and then disappear, just like that?" I started crying again. I waited to hear her once again, but I didn't hear anything.

***

I parked and jumped out of my car. I stumbled to her door and started pounding on the door. "Open up, Amoy," I yelled.

I knew she was there because I saw her car. I wasn't leaving until she opened this damn door.

"What the fuck you doing here, bitch?" She opened the door.

I didn't respond. I used all my force, pushing the door wide open while I stumbled inside, hitting the floor.

"I need to talk to you, Amoy." I tried to regain my balance without further embarrassing myself.

"Bitch, I have nothing to talk to you about. Now get yo ass out of my shit before I throw your drunk ass out." She stood there with an angry look on her face.

"Listen, sis… I know I fucked up. I should've stopped talking to Devon once I found out that was who you were messing with. But by the time I found out, I was already in love with him… My entire life, you have always been the happy one. The one that everybody praised. I was always in your shadow as Amoy's little sister…"

"So what, bitch? You decided to take the same dick that I was fucking? You're fucking disgusting. How do you feel, you fucking the same nigga that I fucked?"

"I'm sorry, Amoy. I swear, if I could go back and change the hands of time, I would never sleep with Devon."

Loving Him Ain't Worth A Damn Part 2

"Well, hoe, it's too late for your sorrys and for you to pretend like you give a fuck. So, why are you really here?"

"I'm pregnant! Mama is not here. You're the only one I've got," I blurted out.

"Ha ha, you're pregnant? Why would I give a fuck? Did you forget all the fucked up ass names you called my child? Bitch, why in God's name would I give a fuck about that motherfucker you're carrying? If you came over here for any kind of pity, you knocked on the wrong bitch's door because you're dead to me. Now get yo ass out of my shit." She walked over to the door and opened it wide.

I was desperate... I didn't know what to do. This bitch wasn't trying to hear me out.

"I'm your sister. This is me, Amoy, Shari, your little sister. Mama is gone now, and we are all we got." I grabbed her arm, trying to hug her.

"Bitch, get the fuck off of me. You're the worst kind of snake. The kind that hides behind that 'sissy' shit. See, I loved you, so I was blind and didn't see the real you until it was too late. As long as I'm living, I would never fuck with you again."

She grabbed my shoulder and pushed me out the door, slamming her door shut.

"Please, Amoy. I need you. I swear I'm sorryyyyy," I cried out.

"Aye, cool down on the noise," her neighbor opened her door saying.

"Bitch, shut the fuck up!" I yelled back.

After minutes of pleading and begging, I realized that she wasn't trying to open the door. I sat up and stumbled out of her building. I was crushed even more. I grabbed my phone and dialed Devon's number, but he still didn't respond.

I sat in my car and pulled out the little pack of cocaine that I had. I'd been dabbling here and there for about a year now, but lately, it had become an everyday thing for me. I put the coke in a dollar bill. I took a quick glance around, to check if anyone was looking. I then snorted the white powder. It only took a few seconds for it to hit my brain. My sullen mood quickly changed as I felt powerful, like I was in control now. I was fully alert now.

I searched my phone for Kennedy's number. I knew she probably wouldn't pick up, but if she did, I planned on letting her know what the fuck her husband had been up to.

"Hello. So you're a bold bitch. Didn't I tell you not to call my phone anymore?"

"Listen, lady. I'm not calling for your husband. I'm calling to talk to you."

"Talk to me? Whatever I had to say to you, I said it the day I visited you. Now go ahead, little girl, before I end up hurting you."

"Ha ha, that's hilarious, but I ain't worried 'bout yo old ass hurting me. But listen, lady, I need to talk to you."

Loving Him Ain't Worth A Damn Part 2

"I am done talking to you. Keep on, I'm going to get you for harassment."

"Kennedy, chill out. Your husband is planning to kill you."

"What?"

"You heard me right… Your husband is going to have you robbed and killed."

"Did you say you want to talk? When can you meet up?"

"I can meet now. You've got the address; meet me at the crib."

"Sure thing."

I hung the phone up and pulled off. I was trying to get to the house before she got there. I was still tweaking, plus the scent of alcohol was seeping through my pores. Not that I gave a fuck, but if I wanted the bitch to believe me, then I needed to not appear like I was high or drunk.

I took a quick shower, brushed my hair into a ponytail, and brushed my teeth. I put on a pair of tights and a wife beater. I looked down and realized my stomach was showing a little bit. Fuck, I'd been so fucked up for the past few days that I didn't have time to worry about being pregnant. Anger crept up on me; that fucking nigga, Devon, didn't give a fuck about me or this baby. I rubbed my stomach. *Oh, well, his loss,* I thought.

Within minutes, I heard the doorbell ringing. I already knew it was her. The bitch kind of made me nervous with her old, evil ass, but tonight, she was my ally. With what I was about to tell her, she was going to love me.

I opened the door, and she walked in. "Ain't nobody follow you here, right?" I asked.

"Why would anyone follow me?"

The truth was, I was still high as fuck off of the powder. I let out a long sigh, trying to control myself and hoping she wasn't smart enough to know I was high as fuck.

"So, let's get to the point. You said on the phone that my husband was planning my murder?"

"Yes, yes, but before I tell you anything, I need some money."

"Hoe, you're silly. Your broke ass thought you were going to extort money from me?" She laughed.

"Listen, lady, chill out wit' the name calling, okay? I think we both know that nigga ain't worth shit. I've got some info, and you've got some money, so I think we can work something out."

"What makes you think I would pay to get information from you when I can just call the police and have them arrest your ass for forgery?"

"Forgery, police… You know what? You can get yo ass out of my shit."

I walked over to my door and opened it up. I was bluffing to see if this bitch was serious.

"How much money are you talking about?"

Loving Him Ain't Worth A Damn Part 2

"Let say about... Hmm, let's see how much this information means to you... Hmm. About ten grand."

"Bitch, you've lost your damn mind. The whole nigga ain't worth that fucking much."

"Take it or leave it... But what I have is juicy, real juicy." I winked at her.

"I'm gone. Don't call my fucking phone no more."

She started to walk off, but I jumped in front of her.

"Stop. Wait, give me five grand, and I'll give you everything, including the recording that I have."

"I say that's a deal. Now tell me what you know and give me the disc, and I will gladly write you a check."

"A check? I need cash. What if your check ain't good?"

"I don't know what kind of people you're used to, but I am a businesswoman. I don't go around writing bad checks. We have a deal."

It took about twenty minutes for me to tell her about Devon's plan to have her murdered. I then gave her the disc that I had recorded Devon on, for security purposes. See, this nigga thought he was so fucking smart, but I was always one step ahead of him. He would learn that I was not to be fucked with.

I watched as she pulled her checkbook out and wrote the check. "Here you go, but before I go, let me ask you a question. Why did you decide to turn against him?"

I grinned at her, looked at the check, and then responded.

"That nigga ain't loyal to nobody but himself, and I'm only loyal to me. That nigga said fuck me, so I'm fucking him raw without grease."

She nodded and walked quietly out of my apartment. I quickly locked my door. I was happy she was gone. There was something about being in that bitch's presence that made my skin crawl. She came off as nice, but I could see the poison pouring out.

I looked at the check and my eyes widened. I hadn't seen this much money in a while. My account was almost drained because I'd been dipping in it to keep up with these bills and even more because I was getting high more than usual. I really needed to get this shit under control soon. I swear I didn't want to turn out like Mama. But Mama was smoking crack; all I was doing was powder...

I grabbed the phone. "Aye, can I come see you?"

"Yeah, I'm around the way."

"Okay, cool. I've got to stop at the bank and I'll be on my way."

I hung the phone up and took out the last little bit of dust I had left. I placed it on a dollar bill and started sniffing it. After the second drag, I was back on cloud nine.

Was that a knock I heard, or was I tripping? I wiped my nose and walked over to the door. *Shit, it's Devon. What is he doing here?*

Loving Him Ain't Worth A Damn Part 2

I was too happy to see my man. I guess he was missing me as much as I was missing him. I quickly opened the door. "Hey, babes." I greeted him in an upbeat mood.

He didn't respond though. He just walked past me and into the living room. I locked the door and followed behind him.

"You okay, babes?"

"What was Kennedy doing here?"

"Huh? Who... what are you talking about, Devon?"

Blap! Blap! Blap!

"Bitch, don't play with me. What the fuck was Kennedy doing up in here?"

"Devon, baby, she wasn't here, or if she was, I didn't see her."

That nigga raised the gun and slapped me a few times, knocking me to the ground. I held my face as I screamed and pleaded for mercy.

"Now what the fuck did you tell her?"

"I didn't tell her anything, Devon. I swear, baby, I would never betray you. Please, baby, don't forget that I'm pregnant."

"Bitch, I don't give a fuck 'bout that bastard or you. Bitch, I told you to leave me the fuck alone, but you didn't listen. I told yo ass."

I balled up in a fetal position as he stomped me. I knew then that he'd come to handle business.

"Please, Devon, please. I swear I didn't tell her nothing," I cried.

His anger was rising as he knelt down and started beating me in the head with the gun. I started losing consciousness. I tried to plead with him, but my mouth was hurting so bad that the words were not coming out. Everything around me started spinning, and the room got darker... I tried to stay awake, but I couldn't. Eventually, I closed my eyes, hoping that when I woke up this would all be a dream...

CHAPTER TEN

Kennedy

Hmm... that was strange. When I left, Devon was at the house. He said he was tired and was lying down. I knew I wasn't gone that long, but his car was gone. I pulled into the garage and got out of the car. I walked up the stairs. I searched through the house to make sure it was empty.

I then locked my room door and put the disc into my computer and played it. Tears rolled down my face as I heard my husband, another man, and that bitch discussing how my murder was supposed to take place. I knew that he was a cheater but never suspected that nigga was also a killer. His words sent chills up my spine when he described to the other man how he wanted it done. I was tearing the fuck up because I'd killed before but this was me that they were discussing.

I heard the door open, so I hurriedly cut the computer off. I pulled out the disc, put it back in the envelope, and threw it back into my purse. I grabbed the mail nearby, so I could pretend like I was reading.

"Hey, love. You're back fast."

"I told you I was only making a quick run. I thought you were taking a nap?"

"Shit, I was until my homeboy hit me up, and I had to go meet him."

"Devon, I hope you're not back in them streets, dealing them drugs again."

"Hell nah, babes. I told you that part of me was over. I ain't goin' lie; I miss making all that money, but I can't risk losing you behind no foolish decision."

"I love you, Devon. I just want us to be happy."

He sat beside me on the bed. "Kennedy, after today, we will forever be happy."

"Why? What happened today that was special?"

"Nothing special happened. Listen, babes, I'm all yours forever."

I didn't respond. Instead, I just rubbed his hand.

***

I was up in the living room, drinking a cup of coffee and watching the morning news on ABC. The reporter came on, talking about the body of a young girl that was found Friday evening after 7 P.M. She went on to say that she was brutally murdered.

"Good morning, babes," I heard Devon holler as he walked down the stairs.

"Hey, love," I yelled back.

My focus, however, was on the news and what the reporter was saying. I spit coffee all over the place when the picture of the bitch that I visited that same evening flashed across the screen.

"Devonnnnn," I yelled out as I stood up.

He ran into the living room. "What's wrong, babe?"

Loving Him Ain't Worth A Damn Part 2

I couldn't even get the words out. I just pointed to the television. He looked and then looked back at me. "Somebody got murdered."

"Not just anybody. The little bitch that you were sleeping around with," I blurted out.

"Really? Well, you know her ass was out there. It was only a matter of time before one of them niggas killed her for playing them."

"Devon, you didn't have nothing to do with this, right? This happened yesterday evening."

"Babe, you're tripping. I ain't no killer. Trust me, I was nowhere near that girl or her apartment."

His tone was cold, but it was his demeanor that grabbed my attention. I didn't believe him. I recalled that, when I came back, he wasn't home. What if he followed me? He would've known that I went to see her.

"Well, babe, now we ain't got to worry about her bothering us no more."

"You're right about that." I smiled at him.

"What's your plan for later?"

"Nothing, do some cleaning and put a roast in the oven for dinner."

"Sounds like a plan. I'ma make some runs, and then I'll be back home to spend some quality time with the wife." He kissed me on my lips.

Racquel Williams

I sat back on the couch. If he saw her after I saw her, did she tell him that I was aware of him plotting my murder? I had too many questions with not enough answers. *Fuck, the check that I wrote her.* My head started spinning.

***

I went ahead and canceled the check. I prayed to God the police didn't find it. I had no idea how I was going to explain why I wrote a check to my husband's side bitch that so happened to end up murdered the same date as the check. I thought about going over there and breaking in, but that was even crazier. I didn't kill the bitch and definitely didn't want to get caught up in no murder investigation.

I went grocery shopping and grabbed the biggest, juiciest looking roast. Tonight was a very special night, and I planned on preparing a big meal. After the grocery store, I stopped at the liquor store and grabbed some Grey Goose. I saw that Devon's liquor of choice was almost gone. I grabbed me a bottle of Remy Martin V. This was becoming one of my favorites.

After I got home, I washed and seasoned the roast and let it marinate for a while before I put it into the oven with carrots and potatoes. It didn't take long for the aroma to fill the entire house. I started drinking early, and before you knew it, I was feeling pretty good. I was in a great mood, and nothing or no one was going to stand in my way ever again. I was just setting the table when I heard Devon enter the house. *Damn, he's home early*, I thought. No worries though.

Loving Him Ain't Worth A Damn Part 2

"Hey, love. Damn, woman, you've got this house smelling good."

"You need to get in the shower while I set this table."

"Yes, ma'am." He ran off upstairs.

By the time he was finished dressing, I had the candles lit and his food dished out. I placed the bottle of liquor on the table. I'd been preparing for this night for a while now. Ever since this nigga played me. I tried over and over to go about this another way, but truthfully, I just wanted this bum gone for good, out of my fucking life.

My thoughts were interrupted when he entered the dining room and took a seat across from me.

"Damn, bae, you went all the way out tonight. What a nigga do to deserve this type of royal treatment?"

I smiled at him as I took a sip of my Remy. This fool still had no idea...

"Man, you put yo motherfucking foot in this roast. Shit's so juicy, it's just melting in my mouth."

He was just eating and smiling from ear to ear, saying all the nice words that he thought I wanted to hear. I just listened and smiled.

"Devon, let me ask you something."

"What's good, babe? You aiight?"

"It's been on my mind lately... Did you ever love me, or were you just after what I've got?"

Racquel Williams

He put the fork down and stared at me. "Yo, B… what the fuck kind of question is that? You're the only woman, outside of my mama, that I ever loved like this. You're my motherfucking heart, yo."

"Devon, if a man loves a woman, he would never cheat on her. At least that's how I was raised. You not only disrespected me, but you dragged me around this town. You know how embarrassed I felt? Even my friends thought I was a laughingstock. I mean, what did I do to you that was so bad? I loved, fucked you, sucked your dick, licked your balls, and gave you everything… but that wasn't enough. You still cheated."

"Yo B… Y-o-o…" He was struggling to get his words out.

"I-I-I ca-n't bre-athe. Kenn-ddy." He tried to get up, but he stumbled.

"Oh my, what's wrong, darling? Did you say you can't breathe?"

He held his throat while gasping for air. I took a seat close to him while he struggled. He looked at me with tears in his eyes. He reached out to touch me, but I moved my foot out of the way.

I then knelt down to where he laid at on the tile. He was now foaming out of his mouth. I rubbed his head. "See, darling, I wasn't so stupid after all. You dogged me for a while and then thought I was one of these dumb ass bitches. Wrong. Anyway, say hi to Travis for me. Let him know this old cow is still alive and kicking." I got closer to him and placed a long kiss on his forehead.

Loving Him Ain't Worth A Damn Part 2

I walked away and left him on the floor. It was only a matter of minutes before he would meet his maker. I poured another glass of Remy. "Cheers to husband number two." I placed the glass in the air before I swallowed the liquor. I tuned out his groaning sounds and focused on how I was going to get rid of him. I'd just taken my last sip of liquor when I heard something.

Bang! Bang! Bang! I jumped up. What the fuck was that? I ran to my door and realized it was the police. My heart started racing, and that was when my ass remembered that Devon's body was still on my dining room floor. I was planning to get rid of him after dark.

I figured they were here to arrest Devon for the murder of that girl. All I had to do was tell them he was not here, and they could get on their merry way. I opened the door, smiling.

"Hello there, Officers. How may I help you all?"

"We have a warrant for your arrest and also a search warrant for your house."

The officer then reached in and grabbed my arm. "Mrs. Guthrie, you're under arrest for the murder of Travis Guthrie."

"What are you talking about? I didn't murder anyone and definitely not my husband. Who is responsible for this madness? I promise, y'all have no idea what y'all are doing."

"Detective, come in here. We have a deceased male on the floor."

They looked at me before they rushed inside. One of the remaining officers led me off to the police car. So these bastards

173

wanted to arrest me for killing a nigga years ago. What fucking evidence did they have? None. I couldn't wait for my lawyer to eat their asses up. I sat in the police car. I saw as other cars pulled up. The coroner also pulled up. I hung my head down. My dumb ass really fucked up this time. I was so caught up in all these different emotions that I didn't notice a man walk up to the car.

"Hello, Kennedy."

My eyes popped open. This couldn't be.

"Christopher, what are you doing here?"

"It's Detective Walden."

"Say what. Christopher? Now is not the time for your silly jokes."

"Mrs. Guthrie, I'm not joking. My name is Detective Walden."

My mouth hung wide open. I looked at his face. He was not joking. Shit, he didn't even look the same. Alarms started going off in my head. Detective. Oh my God. He was undercover, and my stupid ass confessed everything to him. That was when it hit me. After all the years, they were charging me with murder because I told this nigga I killed my husband.

"You bastard! How could you?"

This was the same nigga that I fucked and sucked. Oh my God, this couldn't be...

He didn't say a word. He looked at me, shook his head, and walked towards the house, where the rest of the pigs were.

Loving Him Ain't Worth A Damn Part 2

All I could do was cry. How could the one person that I trusted betray me like that?

CHAPTER ELEVEN

Amoy

I had just dropped my baby off at daycare and was about to head back home, so I could clean up before heading to the hospital to see Marquise. The last few days had been hell for us. It was found out that the gunshots had damaged his tissues and organs. Twice, he went into cardiac arrest; however, doctors were very optimistic on his recovery.

For the first time, I got to meet his mom and the rest of his family. It was sad that we had to meet under these circumstances. I could see the hurt in his mom's eyes when she walked in and saw the condition her son was in.

I'd been praying daily for him, and for hours at a time, I would sit with him, telling him how much I loved him. I begged God every day to protect my baby. I swear I couldn't lose him.

My phone was ringing, but I was mopping the kitchen floor. *Whoever that is is goin' to have to wait,* I thought as I continued doing what I was doing. The phone kept ringing though. I could no longer ignore it, so I put the mop down and dashed over to the couch and grabbed it up. I had four missed calls, all from his sister's number. I panicked immediately and dialed her number back. "Hey, babes, I was..."

"You need to get up here now!" she yelled into the phone.

"Okay," was all I said before I dashed to my room. I grabbed my keys and my purse and sprinted out of the door. My heart was jumping

Loving Him Ain't Worth A Damn Part 2

in my chest as I pulled off in a rush. His sister's voice was that of desperation. I knew in my heart that this wasn't good. I felt the tears, trying to seep out, but I used everything in me to hold them in. "God, please don't take my baby away from me." As soon as I said that, the tears poured down my face. I pressed on the gas and dashed to the hospital. I was pissed off that I had to stop at the stop signs because every little second counted.

I pulled up to the emergency entrance and parked. "Ma'am, you can't park right here. You're blocking the entrance," a parking attendant said.

"Get the fuck out of my way," I said as I dashed into the lobby.

I had no time to wait on the elevator, so I ran up the stairs. My feet were moving, but it seemed like I wasn't going fast enough. My chest started tightening up on me, but I didn't let that slow me down. Finally, I got to the ICU. I dashed to his room.

"Ma'am, no one is allowed in that room right now but the immediate family," the police that was guarding his door said. He was definitely new and not the regular one that had been there.

"She's family. Let her in."

I ran in the room, and I saw the doctors, nurses, and his family standing over him. I looked at them and pushed towards him. His sister grabbed me. "He's gone. My brother is gone," she yelled as she held me in a bear type hug.

Racquel Williams

I looked at her like she was a foreign object. "He ain't gone. My baby's right there. C'mon… Tell them, baby." I tried to break loose.

"Let me go. Let me get to my baby," I yelled at the top of my lungs. I used all of my strength and broke free from her. I dashed over to him and threw my body on him, holding his face. "Baby, c'mon, wake up. I know you're just playing. Wake up, Marquise. Noooooooooooooooooooo," I screamed from the bottom of my lungs.

***

When it rained, it poured. After I left the hospital, on my way home, I got a phone call from the police telling me that my sister was dead. She was found murdered. After I hung the phone up, I pulled over to the side of the road, and I cried. I had no idea if I was crying because she was dead or I was relieved that she would no longer be a nuisance to me. They said God didn't give you more than you could bear, but shit, God must have known by now that I couldn't bear anymore. I lost three people back to back. How was I supposed to carry on like this?

After I got myself together, I pulled back on the road. It was late, and I needed to get my baby home.

I couldn't sleep because I was so used to him being on the other side of the bed. I kept reaching over, just like I used to do. Only this time, he didn't reach back and pull me closer. I had no idea how I was going to live without him. I grabbed the pillow and hugged it close to me, inhaling his strong scent that was all over the pillow.

Loving Him Ain't Worth A Damn Part 2

God, I can't live without him, I really can't... I could still hear him telling me how much he loved me. Who would be so wicked to take my baby's life away? Whoever it was, they were going to pay. I grabbed my cellphone and dialed Devon's number. As I sat there, waiting for his bitch ass to answer, I had no doubt that he was responsible for what happened to Marquise. He didn't answer; instead, his phone just rang out until the voicemail came on.

"Listen up, you little bitch ass nigga. I know you're the one that shot my man. But don't worry; Lady Karma's going to visit yo ass, and when she does, I hope you're fucking ready. I hope you die a slow fucking death. I fucking hate you with everything in me." I hung the phone up and threw it onto the bed.

"God, please take this pain that I'm feeling away from me. I can't live like this, God," I cried out as I collapsed on the floor.

Made in the USA
Lexington, KY
16 June 2018